THIS ONE NIGHT

The one consuming passion of Tona Felton's life has been to travel and forget the monotony of her life as a City typist in London. The dark stranger who made passionate love to her while the Balkan Express thundered across Europe turned out to be a king, but as war clouds gathered over the Balkans and she was herself involved in plot and counter-plot, she fought not for a country, but for love.

THIS ONE NIGHT

This One Night

by

Denise Robins

Dales Large Print Books
Long Preston, North Yorkshire,
BD23 4ND, England.

British Library Cataloguing in Publication Data.

Robins, Denise
    This one night.

    A catalogue record of this book is
    available from the British Library

    ISBN   978-1-84262-647-4 pbk

First published in Great Britain in 1942 by
Hutchinson & Co. Ltd.

Published in Large Print 2009 by arrangement with
Patricia Clark for executors of Denise Robins' Estate

Dales Large Print is an imprint of Library Magna Books Ltd.

Printed and bound in Great Britain by
T.J. (International) Ltd., Cornwall, PL28 8RW

1

In the years before the war the one consuming passion of Tona Felton's life had been to travel, to get away from the monotony of her existence in London and forget about life as a City typist knows it, with its wearing monotony of days filled with work and nights void of any real excitement.

Now as she stood on the crowded platform of Istanbul station she had to laugh at the perversity of fate which had decreed that her nomadic impulses were not to be fulfilled until the world was in the midst of a war which was gradually closing the frontiers of almost every European country which she had wanted to visit. This was no pleasure-seeking holiday crowd which jostled and pushed their way towards the trains. The whole atmosphere was pregnant with a feeling of tense realism as though the people knew they were living on the edge of a volcano which might erupt at any moment to cover them with the relentless lava of war.

So far, Tona decided, she had certainly

experienced more than her fair share of excitement. The convoy in which she had sailed from Tilbury had been attacked by submarine and from the air, and now she found herself at half-past six on a hot summer's evening at one of the largest and busiest junctions in Europe, ready to take her place on the Balkans Express. How thrilling it sounded! The Balkans Express which would speed with her through lovely, unknown lands towards Gardenia.

As far as she had been able to ascertain, she was the only British subject who wanted to go to Gardenia, and when she stood on the platform trying to make her way through the cosmopolitan crowd towards the long gleaming train in the great station, she found herself a stranger amongst a lot of gesticulating, chattering foreigners of apparently every nationality except her own. She was jostled and nudged. Nobody seemed to notice her. At least, so Tona thought, as flushed and breathless she tried to reach one of the second-class carriages in the express, her bag under her arm and a suitcase in each small hand.

She was much too preoccupied and flustered to be aware of the fact that somebody was watching her very intently. Two brilliant blue eyes, which looked all the bluer because of a darkly browned face, had glanced at first idly in her direction, then with intensity.

The eyes belonged to a slimly-built man above average height, and of unusual grace, who was leaning out of a coach at the end of the train.

He spoke in Gardenian to someone who stood behind him.

'Paul, look at that girl, English, obviously. Not particularly chic. But, my dear fellow, have you ever seen such beauty?'

The man called Paul glanced out of the window. He smiled as he saw the girl, who with her two suitcases was pushing and struggling towards the train. Without doubt she was more than ordinarily beautiful. A perfect blonde. One could just glimpse fair, shining hair under the small blue hat; an exquisite figure in the grey tweed travelling coat; a face like a flower.

'She is attractive, Highness,' he agreed.

'I would like to see the colour of her eyes, Paul,' said the young man who had first noticed Tona.

The other smiled again and shrugged his shoulders.

'I envy you, Highness, that you can turn your thoughts to the colour of a woman's

9

eyes, when the affairs of state press one so furiously.'

'There are times when it is good to forget politics and intrigue, Paul, especially when there are such perfect things to concentrate upon as that exquisite creature.'

The elder man nodded his head. He was used to the sudden fancies of his prince. Valentine of Gardenia was a prince of lovers as well as of his beautiful country. He had been educated at an English public-school and had taken a degree at Balliol. With his sun-browned skin and blue eyes he might have been a typical healthy, sport-loving Englishman. Only his blue-black hair gave away the foreign blood. His English was flawless. Whenever he stayed in England there were always women around Valentine. He adored pretty women, flattering them all and loving none of them. But they broke their hearts for him.

Tona Felton, still unconscious of those handsome eyes which were levelled on her, reached the side of the express at the same moment as a bearded man in uniform approached her.

'Tickets, please!'

Tona put down her suitcases. The crowd and the heat were exhausting her. She loved warm weather and had wanted sunshine, but the atmosphere in the glass-roofed station was unbearable. She glanced longingly towards the interior of the train, which looked cool and inviting.

A second later her fair young face turned crimson and her lips opened in a cry of dismay.

'My bag!'

It had gone. There was no doubt about it. The blue leather bag with all her money in it, her keys, and make-up accessories had vanished completely. She could guess at once what had happened. Some thief on the platform must have taken it from under her arm in that seething crowd.

'Tickets!' repeated the official impatiently.

Tona's colour faded. She went white. She began to explain, but the man, who spoke English badly, was insolent and unsympathetic. He intimated that the English 'Miss' was trying to board the express without paying. It was his duty to hand her over to the police. They were accustomed to dealing with such offenders.

Tona protested vehemently.

'I tell you I *had* my ticket for Gardenia. It's been stolen. You can't have me arrested. It would be ludicrous.'

The ticket collector answered her roughly. Tona could see that he was not to be argued with. Her heart sank. Every penny she possessed had been in that bag. If she didn't find it she would be in a hopeless position. Matters looked black. She was frankly terrified by the prospect of being detained in a Turkish prison without knowing a soul to whom she could turn to help her out of her difficulties. If only she would see an English face or hear an English voice.

Then she heard what she imagined *was* one – a rich softly-modulated voice at her elbow.

'Can I be of any assistance?'

A thrill of utter relief shot through her. She looked up into a very brown face from which handsome, laughing eyes looked down at her eagerly.

'It's my bag,' she explained. 'I've lost it. It must have been stolen. This man doesn't believe me. If you can make him understand you, for heaven's sake don't let him hand me over to the police.'

'I most certainly will not,' he said confidently, and turning spoke a few curt words to the official. The man's attitude was transformed. Bowing low, he muttered a stream of apologies and hastened down the platform. 'You see,' Tona added breathlessly. 'I'm going to Gardenia. I shall be all right once I get there. I expect a friend to meet me and I can get some money.'

'You have your passport?'

'Fortunately, yes. In my coat pocket.'

'Then you need worry no more,' said the stranger. 'Please come with me. I can arrange a place for you on the train, in my carriage.'

'It's frightfully kind of you,' Tona stammered. 'If I can just borrow a little money until I get there...'

He smiled down at the distressed young face.

'You shall borrow all you need. What is your name?'

'Felton,' she told him. 'Tona Felton.'

He lifted her suitcases and led the way, and she followed sighing with relief. It was certainly a stroke of luck to find an Englishman here who was so kind and helpful. Incidentally, he was extraordinarily good-looking, she thought. Yes, her lucky star was holding fast. She had once believed it was only on the films that devastatingly handsome young men came to the assistance of maidens in distress.

A moment later she found herself following him through the most magnificent railway coach which she had ever seen. It astonished her. It seemed like *hôtel de luxe*. One luxurious compartment led into another. She glimpsed a bedroom, a dining-car, a drawing-room with gold brocade curtains shutting out the crowded platform. There were flowers everywhere, books, a radio and every modern gadget for the traveller's convenience.

'This certainly isn't second-class!' she exclaimed. 'I've never seen such beautiful fittings. I'd always heard the Balkans Express was a super train – but this–'

'I know you will be comfortable,' the young man said casually. 'I've reserved this suite. I shall be delighted if you will use it until we reach Gardenia.'

Tona paused beside him, a little breathless and uncertain.

'I hardly feel justified in accepting so much.'

'But please,' he broke in. 'There is so much room.'

'It seems presumptuous.'

'Nonsense,' he interrupted again. 'You mustn't refuse. I have helped you. Now won't you do me a good turn and relieve my boredom? I find travelling alone somewhat dull, don't you?'

He gave her a swift smile. It dazzled her strangely. There was extraordinary magnetism in this exceedingly handsome young man in his perfectly-cut grey flannels and well-chosen tie. But her voice was still hesitant when she replied: 'I still don't think I should.'

He nodded towards the platform.

'You can't prefer all that trouble with the authorities and possible arrest. Anyway, I told them you were with me.'

She laughed.

'In that case I'll stay.'

He, too, laughed as though gripped by a sudden curious elation, and turned to walk into the next compartment where the man called Paul sat reading.

'Paul,' he said in an undertone, 'the English lady travels in my suite to Gardenia. See that I am not worried and that she does not know who I am. I will remain incognito. Use the name of Carr.'

The equerry to the Prince of Gardenia rose and bowed.

'The boy is incorrigible,' he thought. 'Will he ever settle down?'

Aloud, he said: 'I understand, Highness.'

Then Valentine gave his equerry one of

15

those dazzling smiles which endeared him to all who knew and served him, men and women alike.

'She is truly wonderful, my dear Paul. Her name is Tona. I like her.'

Paul Lavengro, a member of one of the oldest families in Gardenia, Royalist from all time and fiercely loyal to the throne, looked with mingled affection and sadness towards Valentine. The prince was a charming boy, considerate and kind. But what would be the outcome of these light frothy affairs which meant nothing in the end? One day he must marry, and it must be a princess of the royal blood. No hazel-eyed English girl called Tona could ever mean anything vital or lasting to Valentine of Gardenia. Such affairs were, of course, not so serious so long as they *were* meaningless. But there was always the chance, he reflected, that his beloved prince might one day fall in love and be hurt.

It was a somewhat bewildered Tona who found herself in that small luxurious drawing-room which seemed so unlike a train, drinking a cocktail with her newly-acquired benefactor. His name, he told her, as he busied himself with ice and shaker, was Valentine Carr. He was going to Gardenia

16

for a protracted stay.

'I'm so glad I saw you and was able to help,' he went on, raising a glass to his lips. 'Good luck, and happy days in Gardenia!'

'Thank you. Good luck!'

'Now, do please take off your hat and coat. It's warm in here.'

'Yes, it is,' she agreed. 'But it's heaven compared to that sweltering station.'

Valentine sat down opposite her, and watched her remove her things. He had told Paul that she was not 'chic,' but he had never seen a girl more beautifully built, with that slim, straight line which he admired; straight wide young shoulders and narrow waist and the smallest of ankles and well-bred hands and feet. Her dress – grey, with a white organdie collar – was charming. His gaze narrowed as it rested on the smooth, shining waves of her hair. What a lovely child she was! Obviously in her early twenties. He liked the way that fair hair was cut and curled under in a page-boy 'bob' at the nape of the slender neck. He wondered if a lover's lips had ever brushed the tiny gold tendrils clustering there.

'Tell me about yourself,' he said.

Tona sat down and smiled. She found it remarkably easy to talk to this young man.

17

The train was already moving out of the station, but the coach was so perfectly sprung that she scarcely felt any vibration as they passed over the points. She looked with shining eyes around the miniature *salon,* at the artistically arranged flowers, the heavy rugs on the floor and the gold and purple cushions on the sofa.

'This is thrilling,' she said. 'It's like a scene out of … a film.'

'You make it all very thrilling for me,' he said.

She gave him a quick look, then changed colour, and her long, thick lashes dropped. He could see that she had the typical English girl's shy reserve. The shyness intrigued him. He repeated: 'Tell me about yourself.'

She told him something about her life as a typist in a London office. Her parents were dead. She lived with a married sister in Norwood. All her life she had wanted the colour and romance which only travel could supply. She had seen pictures and read books about Gardenia. She was sure that it was an enchanted country. For many months she had saved in order to take a holiday there. Now she was going on business. Her firm had important papers which had to be taken to their agent in Gardia, the capital, and she was the only member of the staff who could be spared to contact him. It was a stroke of luck for which she would always be thankful.

'It seems strange,' she added, 'that it should take a war to get me to my peacetime Utopia.'

He watched her closely, thinking what a waste of youth and beauty it was for such a girl to be shut up in the drab surroundings of a city office. She was so obviously sensitive to beauty and colour. Her mind was as responsive as a violin string. It was disagreeable to Valentine to think of such a mind being dulled, perhaps by marriage to some uninspired young man who would wear a blue suit on Sundays and keep his money in a little pouch purse. She was too good to spend her life cooking midday dinners in a 'homely' and suburban villa.

'You say you know somebody to whom you can go in Gardia?' he asked.

Tona nodded.

'Yes. His name is George Oliver.'

Valentine's handsome face puckered a little.

'Who is he? Your fiancé?'

She shook her head vigorously. No, George was not her fiancé, she laughed. He was the agent of whom she had spoken. But they had known each other for years. He used to work beside her in the London office. He had often asked her to marry him and she liked him, but she didn't love him. But he had promised to look after her and give her a good time in Gardia. That was all.

'I see,' said Valentine. He lit a cigarette and the smoke hid the momentary spark of relief in his eyes. 'Can it be possible that you have no man in whom you are, shall we say, interested?'

She gave another embarrassed little laugh.

'It's not only possible, but a fact. I've never met any man who appealed to me – in that way.'

'But if you did find somebody who appealed to you – it would be exciting, wouldn't it?'

'It probably would be,' she agreed, and was suddenly afraid of those brilliant, attractive eyes which watched her so closely.

He thought: 'How sweet she is! Totally unspoiled. She would love well – *when she loved...*'

His gaze moved to her lips. Tona's mouth was curved for kisses. It was red and ripe. As passionate and promising as those great hazel-gold eyes. Yes, there was passion and promise in her face, in exciting contradiction to the cool reticence of her manner which so intrigued him.

Why, he wondered, should this little English typist so disturb Valentine of Gardenia who had a world of beautiful, *soignée* women to choose from? So often in his life he had loved like the gypsy and ridden away. But this evening as the Balkans Express sped through the gathering dusk on its all-night journey to Gardenia a queer feeling of unrest gripped him. A feeling that he no longer wanted to go on philandering. That he would like to have taken this unspoiled, charming child away from the world and stayed with her – always.

But that, of course, was mere day-dreaming. A throne, a crown, a country in the heart of the Balkan cockpit and a royal marriage were his destiny.

And Tona thought of the last conversation which she had had with her sister and brother-in-law, the evening before she started out for Gardenia. She had a swift vision of the poky little house which was not far from the ruins of the old Crystal Palace (one of the excitements of their lives had been watching that spectacular fire). She could see the 'lounge' which Kathleen had

21

tried to furnish in modern style when she married Tom, who worked in a small wireless shop in the district. She could see Kathleen, fair and once pretty like herself, but washed out, almost haggard at the young age of twenty-five after four years of work in the house. Cook-general's work without pay as she used to complain, and Tom never getting any further. They had been discussing Tom's holidays and Kathleen had suggested a week at Brighton. That had seemed enough to satisfy her. But when Tona had told them she was going abroad for her firm, both Kathleen and Tom had said that it was foolish of her to have taken on the job. Kathleen had said more than that.

'Tom and I don't approve of you going to this outlandish place by yourself in the middle of a war. You'll get into some sort of trouble, and if you do it won't be any use whining to us. You should take the advice given you; hand in your notice.'

Tona had smiled and soothed Kathleen down. Poor old Kathleen! Marriage to a poor and struggling man seemed to have soured her, and Tom was a dull sort of a prig. All the years that Tona had shared their home she had secretly sworn never to give up her freedom for a life of drudgery and monotony such as Kathleen had to endure.

But Kathleen was like their father who had been a dull and unimaginative man. And Tona was her mother all over again. Her poor young mother who had started life on the stage. There were photographs of her at Tona's age. She had been a radiant golden-haired dancer. But she had fallen in love with one of the stage electricians who used to stand in the wings and watch her dance. And she had married him and renounced her career, and with it all the laughter and the dancing. For her portion had been like Kathleen's – hard work and no pay, and two little girls to bring up into the bargain. She had died of pneumonia when she was still in her thirties and Tona just sixteen. Their father had followed her to the grave tragically a few months later, victim of a street accident. And after that the two girls had had to fend for themselves.

So they had no legacy except misfortune and privation, and Tona had worked for her living from the day she left school. The day after her father's death. She had attended a Pitman's school and learnt to be a short-hand typist. And soon afterwards, Kathleen, who was older, had married Tom, and told

23

Tona she was lucky to share a home with them.

But Tona didn't think she was lucky. She had her mother's temperament. A love of drama. A natural inclination for gaiety … a desire for colour and romance. She did not wish to share the fate of her poor little disappointed mother, or of Kathleen who slaved and groused all day. But so far she had had no chance to spread her wings. She had just carried on with her job in the City, travelled back to the house in Norwood every evening and spent most of her week-ends doing her share of the work and washing. Until now…

And now had come this wonderful opportunity to travel for her firm to their agency in Gardia. Tona's firm supplied artificial flowers which were made in the Gardenia factory. There had been some muddle in ledgers and accounts, and Tona, who had been with the firm for the last three years and knew her job, had been detailed off to carry the ledgers and correspondence over to the Continent and straighten out the tangle personally with George Oliver. A commission which made her rightly proud.

And this was the beginning of her adventure. A breathless and brilliant beginning,

24

she told herself, as she watched Valentine Carr.

Who was he, really, she wondered. Where did he come from? He was no ordinary person. Of that she was sure. And she told herself to be careful. His words were flattering and he was dangerously handsome. It was obvious that he was used to saying pretty things to many women. She had allowed him to befriend her, but she must be on her guard, not only against him, but against herself.

A black-coated servant entered the *salon*.

'When will you dine, sire?'

'At eight-thirty,' said Valentine. 'Lay the table for two.'

The man bowed and retired. Tona, who had not been able to understand a word, said: 'What did he say, Mr Carr?'

Valentine thought how deliciously she used that name. He was so weary of being addressed as 'Highness.' It was particularly pleasing to listen to her.

'He asked about dinner. I've ordered it for us both at half-past eight.'

Her heart-beats quickened. Was she to make the journey entirely alone with this attractive stranger?

'Are you sure it's no trouble?'

He leaned towards her.

'Quite sure. You won't deny me the pleasure of your company, will you?'

She found herself saying no. For some unaccountable reason she could not refuse him. But looking once again into those brilliant, penetrating eyes, she thought: 'Tona, my girl, don't lose your head. This is pure Hollywood. You must be careful.'

When they had finished their drinks Valentine showed her the way to a charming little sleeping-compartment. Like the rest of the coach, it was superbly furnished. A bowl of scarlet carnations stood on the perfectly appointed dressing table. There were photographs of several attractive women – some of them signed in English: *'To Val.'* Others, in Gardenian, which baffled Tona.

She looked at the photographs a trifle ironically. She had been right in her conjecture, she thought. The fascinating Mr Carr was the type of man who must have met and been sought after by many women. From now on she would accept his most flattering remarks with the reserve for which they called. She began to protest that this was his own private compartment.

'I can't *possibly* turn you out,' she said.

He shook his head.

'There is another in my suite. You must have this one. I insist. Do please use it for tonight. Now you would like to wash and change your frock for dinner. I'll join you in the *salon*.'

He closed the door behind him. Tona gasped a little. He was very dictatorial, this young man. It was obvious that he was accustomed to having his own way. Well, that was easy when you had limitless money, as apparently he had. She only hoped, for his own sake, that he was not thoroughly spoiled.

She glanced at the photographs of the pretty smiling women – some in *décolleté* – some in handsome furs – one or two in sports suits – and smiled. What stories of glamorous Balkan nights could they tell? What easy word of love had 'Val' whispered to them? She remembered his soft lazy voice saying: 'If you did find somebody who appealed to you – it would be thrilling, wouldn't it?'

She caught her breath. She was suddenly deliciously terrified. She had craved life and romance. Today she had fallen straight into it as the guest of this strangely attractive man with whom she was speeding through the night towards Gardenia.

The next moment she found herself half-wishing she had never accepted his help. She did not know a thing about him, save that he was exactly the type of man who appealed to her vitality. A masterful, challenging, dominating personality.

She put a hand on the handle of the door, as though to rush out of the sleeping compartment into the other *salon* and tell Mr Carr that she could not remain in his suite. The train roared on through the moonlit country and she swayed a little unsteadily on her feet. Then came the sound of a violin being played and of a man's voice. A new thrill of excitement swept through Tona. She knew that tune and the meaning of the words which Valentine was singing. It was a sensuous gypsy melody which held all the magic and fire of the Magyars. The words were a lover's plea to his beloved.

Tona turned away from the door, her eyes darkening with doubt and anticipation. Valentine Carr was sufficiently dangerous by himself. Combined with that romantic Magyar music, he would be devastating. Very slowly she began to change her frock.

2

It was nine o'clock. The Balkans Express had left Istanbul far behind. The long train wound like a glittering serpent through the darkness.

The short brocade curtains in the drawing-room of Valentine's suite were parted so that the sky was visible. A sky that blazed with stars. It was a warm, star-spangled night.

Tona sat on the sofa, listening to the music which came from the finest portable radio-gramophone which money could buy. The record was *Sárga rózsa,* played by Magyari Imre and his gypsy orchestra. The man whom Tona knew as Valentine Carr sat beside her smoking a cigarette in a long holder. He wore a dinner-jacket, and she thought how brown his face looked against the soft white shirt and collar. She was just beginning to notice how black his thick hair was – unusually black for an Englishman.

She was glad she had been somewhat extravagant with her packing and brought one smart evening dress for the trip. She knew she looked her best in it. The man beside her scarcely took his gaze from her face. The severely dressed office-girl had quite vanished. Here was a beautiful *soignée* young woman. Her skin looked lily-white and her hair was pure gold in the soft light. She was adorable in that long black evening skirt which reached her slender ankles, and the little black taffeta coat, relieved by a great bunch of artificial violets. He would like her to be wearing real violets, he thought. Her feet in the black satin sandals looked small enough to stand on the length of his hand. She wore a necklace of old twisted gold around her neck, a gypsy chain, she told him, which had belonged to her grandmother.

They had eaten a perfectly-served dinner, alone and undisturbed. Paul Lavengro, obeying his prince's orders, had vanished discreetly. When they were drinking their coffee and liqueurs Valentine said: 'I wonder if you realise how lovely you are?'

Tona laughed. But there was a trace of coldness in her voice when she replied.

'You say that too easily, Mr Carr.'

Her answer enchanted him. He was used to women who melted under his first smile. He did not flatter Tona again at the table. He talked to her gaily and wittily and made her laugh at his jokes. He told himself that of all the women he had ever known this golden-haired child was the most refreshing.

He knew that he ought to leave her alone – leave her to her dreams and illusions. But before half that evening was over he was staggered by the realisation that he had fallen madly in love with her, and that he had made up his mind that he, and no other man, should teach her what love meant. He would teach her with his heart beating wildly against hers, and his lips brushing the sweet warmth of that inexperienced rose-red mouth of hers.

'Are you really enjoying this?' he asked her when dinner was over and they were back in the *salon* listening to the gramophone. 'You like this music?'

'I love it,' she said. 'I have a lot of Imre's records at home.'

He nodded his approval. Magyari Imre, he told her, was the gypsy violin king who played at the celebrated Marcus Restaurant in Budapest. Nobody visited the town without going to hear him play. The gypsy was a strange-looking person, enormously fat with puny legs, who would often walk far away from his orchestra during a long, slow *lassu* until the others would steal up quietly behind him to support the harmony.

'You should try to go to Budapest to hear him,' Valentine said. 'You would never forget it.'

She nodded.

'It would be wonderful. I might persuade George to take me.'

He moved his dark boyish head impatiently.

'You speak a great deal of this fellow, George. Yet you tell me there is no more than friendship between you.'

Her pulses quickened, but she frowned.

'Have you any objection if I speak of him?'

'I'm inclined to be jealous.'

'*Jealous!*' she repeated, and coloured. 'Isn't it rather absurd to be jealous of someone you have only known a few hours?'

'A few hours is long enough. A mutual attraction can bring two people together like a lightning flash.'

His words thrilled her, but she kept her fair head proudly high.

'I think you are talking rather foolishly.'

'Do you?' he said, half-amused, half-annoyed.

'How many women do you make love to?' she said, laughing again. 'Your bedroom is full of photographs signed: *"To Val."* It amuses me.'

'Do I amuse you?' Suddenly Valentine threw away his cigarette and caught her hand tightly. 'Tell me...'

'Please don't, Mr Carr.'

'You said "Val" so charmingly just now. Say it again.'

'Please,' she repeated, and drew away startled and breathless, her wide eyes clouding.

'I've had many women friends,' he said in a low voice, letting go of her hand. 'I don't deny it. But they have meant nothing. They were mere incidents. Do you believe me, little Goldhead?'

'Why call me such a ludicrous name?'

'It suits you. The colour of your hair is pure heaven in this light.'

'I wish you wouldn't say these childish things.'

'My dear,' he said, laughing softly. 'Don't be mid-Victorian with me. We're in the Balkans, not under the shadow of the Albert Memorial. This is a summer's night. A night of stars and moonshine. I want to see the stars reflected in your eyes. Look at me...'

She tried to get up, her cheeks hot and flaming, her heart beating furiously. She knew she was crazy to allow him to speak to her like this, but somehow he was weaving a spell around her. This warm, luxurious, lamp-lit compartment, full of the perfume of flowers. this romantic flight across the Balkan plains in this wonderful train, this handsome dominant man alone with her – everything combined to break down her defences. She knew it and was frightened, yet enthralled.

'I was enjoying the journey so much,' she said, at last. 'Why spoil it for us both?'

'Don't be angry with me,' he said. 'Don't be. I'm lonely. So tired of the world, of my particular world, if only you knew it, Tona.'

She put a hand to her throat.

'Why should you be lonely and tired?'

'I can't explain. But I am. We're all prisoners of life. My chains happen to be particularly strong. Don't you also get tired of shackles in your life?'

'Yes,' she admitted.

'Then let us both forget our bonds and be happy for a while. Let us snatch our happiness while we may,' he said in a low, deep voice, taking her hand in his and pressing it to his mouth. His lips burned her, travelling up her wrist to her slim bare arm.

The colour drained from her face. No

man had ever made her feel this wild emotion.

'You say you are lonely and tired,' she protested. 'Wouldn't it be more accurate to say you are spoiled? You seem to have everything to make you so.'

'Don't fight against me,' he pleaded. 'You're trembling like a little white moth. Don't bruise your wings against me, darling. There *have* been other women in my life and in my arms. Never one like you. I swear it. You madden me. Your cool reticence makes a flame of me. Turn your face to mine, Tona. Let me look at you...'

She felt powerless to move or speak. Her frightened eyes looked up into his. She managed to gasp: 'You must be insane!'

'I've always been a little insane, darling,' came his laughing reply. 'Some day you may find out the reason for my madness.'

'Who and what are you?'

'Just a man, my dear, who has fallen terribly in love with a golden-haired girl whose name is Tona.'

'Let me go,' she said, thrusting him away.

She wished desperately that he would allow her to leave, for she was not only afraid of him and of his strange, compelling personality – but of herself. She was drowning in a sea of enchantment and she felt, as the Balkans Express rushed through the night, that she was being impelled towards a strange, exotic world from which there might be no release.

She made an effort to pull herself together and regain her mental equilibrium by concentrating on home, on the staid, stuffy little house in Norwood; on Kathleen, her conventional and prosaic sister, the office and George Oliver, an ordinary, rather common man who wanted to marry her. But she could think of nothing but this unique and fascinating young man who was feverishly kissing her hands and arms and sweeping her off her feet with tempestuous lovemaking.

'Tona,' came his urgent voice again. 'You and I are alone. The night is before us. Aren't you going to let it be the most perfect and unforgettable one of our lives?'

He pulled her gently into his arms. She felt his long sensitive fingers threading through her hair, touching her throat and shoulders. Then she realised that an arm was drawing her dangerously close, and that mingling with the roar of the great express was the sound of a gypsy love-song on the gramophone.

The words beat in Tona's brain.

'...I do not ask when summer shall come, nor how long my life shall last; I only ask when I shall belong to my lover...'

Tona shivered.

'Now I know you're mad,' she said, pressing her hands against his shoulders. But once again the hands were caught and carried to Valentine's lips.

'Mad – if love is a madness,' he whispered. 'When you love me you will understand.'

Now she was sealed fast in his arms. She had no resistance left. Her last vestige of control snapped and vanished when she felt his heart beat against her own. She would never forget the magic of those arms, and of those lips which brushed her lashes and strayed to her quivering mouth. He was a wonderful, masterful lover. There could never have been, there could never again be such a lover. But even in the burning glow of this new-found ecstasy, she found herself wondering how many other women had been drowned and lost like this in the storm of his passion.

She heard his voice against her ear, telling her that never again would he want to love or kiss any other woman on earth. His voice carried conviction, but she struggled against the temptation of believing his words.

'You know you don't really care,' she cried. 'Why do you try to make me believe in you?'

He tilted back her chin and looked straight into her eyes.

'I do care. I swear it. The other women do not count. They were too easily loved. You are different.'

'And you're trying to make me like them! You want me to become another "incident".'

'Don't say that. You could never be like the others. When you came into my life today I knew everything would be different – that there could be no other woman but you.'

He meant it. Valentine of Gardenia had met his heart's desire. In some strange, unaccountable way this unspoiled English girl had touched his heart as no other woman had done. He knew that he could not love any woman for ever. His wife must be a royal princess who would eventually share his throne. He knew that he was being selfish and relentless in drawing the very soul out of this girl tonight, and that she, not he, would suffer most. But for the moment he forgot his position; everything was obliterated by this new, wonderful emotion which was sweeping into his life.

'You can't expect me to believe you' she was telling him.

He appeared to ignore her words.

'You are going to love me as much as I love you,' he said. 'Say it, Tona. Say it...'

'I'm afraid.'

'You have no need to be. I will look after you – guard you like the precious jewel you are.'

'No,' she said breathlessly.

But she felt defeated by love, by a passion such as she had not deemed possible. Held fast in his arms, she felt his breath against her face. She was intoxicated. And she knew she must surrender, that now there could be no drawing back for her.

'I adore you,' he said, kissing her throat.

'That doesn't give you the right to expect my love.'

'It must and shall,' he broke in. The handsome, boyish face was now the face of a supplicant, no longer arrogant and demanding. 'Be kind to me, Tona. I'm so weary of pretence. I want something real in life, something vital like this love which you will give me. You're sweet, good, like a flower. I want that flower to wear against my heart for ever.'

'For ever?'

He pressed her gently back on the sofa and placed a cushion under her fair head. Then he bent towards her, his lips against her cheek.

'Yes, for ever. You know you want me. That is why your heart beats so. You are not frightened. You want my love.'

'Val!'

She stammered his name wildly, and as though unable to see or hear, put out a groping hand and touched his thick, dark hair.

"I only ask when I shall belong to my lover."

He quoted the words huskily, covering her face with kisses.

'Tona, you were born for love. For a lover. And that lover had to be myself. Darling, we are going towards heaven tonight as well as to Gardenia.'

She was beyond answering him now. And suddenly he reached up a hand and switched off the light. The *salon* was plunged in darkness. The moonlight streamed through the small windows of the coach, turning Tona's hair to silver. Once again, as he kissed that silver veil of hair, she spoke his name.

'Val...'

'Yes, my Tona,' she heard him say. 'You are going to be mine. You are going to belong to me. You are going to belong to me – now.'

Then she felt herself being lifted into his arms. She knew that she loved him completely and at the same time was aghast at the relentlessness of such love. But she was no longer herself. She was his. All of her. And she wanted him to go on holding her to him and kissing her like this – for ever.

The music played on, until there was only silence, save for the broken, sweet whisperings of love and laughter, and heaven revealed to a golden-haired girl lying in the arms of a princely lover.

3

For Tona, that long night in the Balkans Express was to be unforgettable and wildly sweet. Her most vivid recollection was clinging to Valentine and covering his dark, handsome head with the kisses he had taught her to give.

'You really love me, Val?' she whispered, time and again. 'You are sure of it?'

And he, holding her close, whispered back: 'I shall love you for ever. This is unlike anything else in my life, sweetness, I swear it.'

He meant it. This night was a revelation to Valentine. He meant that he loved this young English girl and that she was necessary to his life. He had always sought and longed for real love and now he had found it.

In the early hours of the dawn he was still awake and thinking of the happiness which had come to him. It was only a few hours before the train was due to arrive at Gardenia's capital, when somebody knocked on the door. Valentine jumped to his feet to answer. The train had halted at some country station which he could see standing silent and deserted against a rolling plain.

He flung open the door and spoke to the man who stood outside.

'What do you want? Why do you disturb me at this hour?'

The man bowed and handed over an envelope.

'A message for you, sire.'

Valentine's eyes narrowed.

'Sire!' he repeated slowly. 'Why do you address me as "sire"?'

The man hesitated for a moment before he answered in a low, grave voice.

'The King of Gardenia is dead. Long live the King!'

Valentine's face went pale in the dawn-light. He staggered a little and leaned against the door.

'My father! You mean my father is dead?'

'I do, sire.' The man spoke rapidly in Gardenian. 'He died yesterday evening. You have to return instantly. I came here by air. The 'plane is waiting for you. We should be at the castle in an hour's time.'

Valentine turned and looked towards a door, the door behind which his golden-haired Tona lay sleeping, his Tona who had lain in his arms happy with love and to whom he had said: *'I love you. I will never leave you. You belong to me utterly.'*

'I can't come just now,' he said over his shoulder. 'Surely a few hours won't make any difference.'

The answer was grave and significant.

'Sire, your people await you.'

Valentine made a superhuman effort to pull himself together.

'You are right, my friend,' he replied dully. 'I will join you outside in a few minutes.'

He crossed the compartment noiselessly to where Tona lay, and stood looking down at her. His eyes were strained, his lips twisted as though with pain. He whispered: 'How was I to know, my darling? How was I to know this would happen?'

He stood there a king, a serious man with grave responsibilities; no longer the gay, carefree boy who had held Tona close to him whilst he spoke tender words of love in her ear. He knew now that no matter how much he loved and wanted her, she was not for him. A throne and a princess were to be his prizes in life's lottery.

Somehow or other he must see her again and try to make her understand, but he realised that because of political matters, he

44

must remain *incognito* and keep his identity hidden until he had crossed the frontier into his own country.

He put a hand across his eyes as though undecided what to do, then picked up a pen and began to write. It would be kinder not to wake her. He would say as much as he could in a letter which she would get in the morning.

He knew that when he left Tona he would be leaving the one woman on earth whom he had ever really loved and for whom he could willingly have forsaken any ambition. He felt morally responsible for her now, but a sterner duty called which must obliterate any personal consideration. He belonged to Gardenia and to his people.

For the first time in his life Valentine, who had found the world a laughing adventure, suffered real anguish. This was the hardest and most painful decision which he had ever been called upon to make.

Without waking Tona, he knelt and kissed her hair. Her face looked exquisitely pure and young in the pale light of the dawn.

'Good-bye, my sweet,' he whispered. 'Forgive me. I'll see you again one day. I must. If and when I can...'

On the platform a small group of men

45

stood in respectful silence. They bowed low as Valentine approached, and after a few words of sympathy and welcome hurried towards a field behind the platform where the aeroplane was waiting.

Valentine climbed into the cabin and looked towards the train which had already begun to steam slowly out of the station. It seemed impossible that twelve short hours should have so devastated his life and hopes. Last night he had found a love which could have borne him to an everlasting pinnacle of bliss. A love which only a throne and a crown could have taken from him. Now he was leaving it all behind. He was setting out on the first stage of a life which could no longer be called his own.

Tona's name was still on his lips when the aeroplane taxied across the field, and with a sudden roar from its engines rose into the sky and turned towards the country which awaited its new ruler.

When Tona awoke the sun was streaming brightly through the window of her sleeping-compartment in Valentine's suite. The sky was a perfect blue across which an occasional fleecy cloud was fanned by a gentle breeze. A warm haze hung over the fields and valleys and crept along the banks of the streams and rivers where cattle and sheep were drinking.

Tona rubbed her eyes lazily and looked towards the open door which led to Val's apartments. He was not there. The rooms were quiet and deserted. A moment later she sat up, her heart pounding and the blood rushing violently to her cheeks as memory after memory of last night returned to her. A scorching blush seemed to envelop her whole body. Fear and ecstasy gripped her. What had she done? She loved this man, but she did not know that love could be so vital, so absorbing, so potent a thing. And he loved her. He had sworn it, promising never to leave her or let her regret.

He would be waiting for her in the *salon*, she decided, and dressing quickly hurried along the corridor. As she went she saw a moving panorama of rich green pasture-land, blue mountains towering against the sky and quaint, white buildings which told her they must be nearing the borders of Gardenia.

'Val!' she called, opening the door. But once again it was only to find the room empty and silent. Suddenly she felt a strange chill of foreboding. Her nerves were tense and she started violently at the sound of a footstep behind her. When she swung round it was to find the servant who had waited on them at dinner. The man bowed and handed her a note. She stared at it and the colour left her face. It could only be from Val. But why? Where was he? What had happened while she was sleeping?

Then she knew. In horror and despair she read what Valentine had written. Of his despair she knew little.

'My sweet. When you read this I shall be gone. I can't explain why, but I got off the train at Fulvia. Try not to think too badly of me. One day you may understand. Please believe that I love you and that I will do so all my life. I am distraught, my Tona, but the memory of you and of last night is unforgettable. Val.'

Twice she read it, her eyes dark and burning, her body ice-cold. Then she flung herself down on the sofa, the sofa on which he had sat with her last night and intoxicated her with his love-making. Her mind was a whirl of doubts and fears. Her first reaction was that she had been a fool to believe in and trust herself to him. Valentine Carr had known many women. Probably he only loved her lightly as he had loved the rest. This note meant nothing.

His love and the memory of last night had left her with a great longing for him, but this morning, believing herself callously deserted, she was horrified by the thought of every kiss he had given her and which she had returned.

'*I shall love you for ever,*' he had whispered against her lips. Yet he had stolen away like a thief in the night, before she was awake. He had left the train at Fulvia, as though too much of a coward to face her.

The rest of the journey to Gardia, Gardenia's capital, seemed interminable. Everywhere Tona looked there was something to remind her of Val and the hours they had spent together. There was the table at which they had dined, the gramophone on which he had played his records of haunting gypsy music, the silver lighter with which he had lit her cigarettes. Even the noise of the wheels rattling over the points seemed to reiterate his name with deadly significance.

She told the servants to leave her alone, saying that she did not wish to eat or drink. She had no desire to come in contact with them or be seen by them more than was necessary. She was too sunk in misery to think of questioning them about Valentine

Carr. At the moment her one ambition was to get off the train and try to get some relief from its painful associations.

It was exactly seven o'clock when the Balkans Express ran into Gardia's main station. Tona expected that George Oliver would be there to welcome her, and soon she saw him standing on the busy platform, searching the long line of carriages with his eyes. She braced herself for the ordeal of their meeting, and a moment later he was beside her, holding her hand and looking at her with frank curiosity.

'Tona, my dear. It's grand to see you. But what's the matter? You look absolutely played out.'

She avoided his gaze.

'Nothing's the matter, nothing at all. How are you George?'

'Oh, not too bad. One lives well and cheaply out here, you know, and a bachelor can have a good time. Fun in the capital and plenty of shooting and fishing up in the mountains.'

She forced a smile.

'It sounds wonderful.'

'Although,' he added, 'one gets a bit sick of this place. It's a bit picture-postcard and *Prisoner of Zenda,* and all that. Look at that porter ... he's like our policemen here, straight out of musical comedy.'

Tona continued to smile as she looked at the porter who was carrying her luggage. A handsome enough lad in an olive green tunic, black gaiters and wearing a green cap with a silver badge on it, on the side of his curly head. Certainly different from the stolid and uninspired railway officials to whom she was accustomed at home.

George Oliver walked beside her, pointing out the famous chiming clock in the central station and the domed roof which was clear crystal and cleaned regularly so that the sun sparkled upon it like a million diamonds. It was all clean and colourful and loud-speakers blared the railway timetable in a language which Tona could not understand. There were crowds of people, a sprinkling of peasants. The women, attractive, with voluminous striped skirts and frilled muslin fichus. The men in corduroy trousers and white cotton blouses.

It would all have been so thrilling, she thought dully, if things had not been as they were on the journey ... if there had been no Valentine Carr.

George pressed her arm against his side as they walked through the booking hall.

'It's grand to see you out here, Tona. I didn't think they'd send you to clear up the mess. I thought they'd send that old stodge, Miss Peebles.'

'Miss Peebles is in hospital having an operation, so I was the one who knew most about the accounts and orders after her.'

'You're as lovely as ever, but you don't look too well,' observed the man.

And that was putting it mildly, he thought. The girl looked positively ghastly and there was a wild sort of look in her eyes. Not at all the cool easy-going little Tona whom he remembered in the office.

She had worked for him the first two years that she was in the firm, and before he was sent out to Gardenia as manager, he had tried hard to get her to marry him. She had refused, but he had put that down to the fact that she was so young. Not yet ready for love and marriage. But he had written to her regularly, always hoping that one day she would change her mind.

Tona looked at her old friend and admirer without enthusiasm. There was nothing particularly romantic or inspiring in George Oliver's appearance, but he was a good-looking man, in his thirties, with brown hair, reddish-brown eyes and close-clipped moustache. He looked what he was, a successful business-man, and typically British in his grey flannel suit.

Life had been easy lately for Oliver. He had worked hard in his slow, plodding way until he had secured a comfortable income and position.

'It's nice to see you, too, George,' Tona said. 'I'm sorry I look such a frightful wreck...'

'But what's happened?' he broke in. 'Are you ill?'

Her gaze fell before his. A dull colour burned her cheeks.

'I've had rather a terrible experience, George. Don't ask me about it here. Let's go straight to my hotel, shall we? This heat is frightful.'

'Very well, my dear.'

He did as she asked. He could not guess what had happened, but if she were in diffi-culties and needed him he would be ready to help her. She had always been a queer, cold little thing, so elusive and beyond his reach that it pleased and flattered him to think she might confide in him, or needed him in any way.

Waiting for the cab to drive up, Tona looked around her, blind to the beauties of the glorious old town which now faced her.

He, himself, had rooms nearer the office. Tona had no interest in her surroundings, she was haunted by thoughts of Valentine, wondered once again what she was going to do, how she was going to blot out the memory of last night. She was filled with a hundred contradictory emotions. She hated Val. She adored him. She never wanted to see him again, she longed for one glimpse of him at the same moment. It was all a hopeless muddle in her emotional young heart.

They reached the hotel and a porter took her luggage. She did not bother to go up and look at her room, but sat on a terrace which looked over a narrow street, and let Oliver take charge of her. He ordered a long cooling drink and gave her a cigarette. He could speak a few words of Gardenian and ordered the servant about in a somewhat fussy and pompous manner. She remembered George had always annoyed her by being pompous. But she was so tired that she allowed him to fuss and was glad of the drink and attention.

This part of the town appeared before her confused and weary gaze like a page from *The Arabian Nights*, combining the warm colours of the Turk with the modelled simplicity of the Greek. The hotel stood on the angle of a curious, straggling street, filled with a noisy, chattering crowd. Exactly underneath the terrace where they were sitting she could see a group of gypsy flower-sellers offering great bunches of multi-coloured blooms to seemingly uninterested customers. The tall houses had narrow latticed windows and wrought-iron bal-conies. The shops leaned from the shadows beneath a sky of translucent blue against which all other colours were contrasted in varying tones. The air was full of the sound of strange cries of vendors, of the clop-clop of horses' hooves on the cobbled roadways.

Tona took off her hat and pushed back a heavy wave of golden hair from her pale young face. Then she added: 'I suppose I'd better tell you – everything, George. It's so on my mind…'

'Yes,' Oliver nodded, 'You must. You know how I feel about you, Tona.'

She shuddered. The last thing she wanted was to remember what any other man might feel or have felt about her. She wanted to forget that such a thing as love existed. She was paying now for the love which a blue-eyed, brown-faced man had given her in his strong young arms last night.

Slowly and deliberately she told George

Oliver what had happened. Her cheeks were on fire, her eyes full of stormy tears as she related the whole story. She began with her arrival at Istanbul station, her lost bag, her meeting with Valentine Carr who had come to her rescue, and insisted that she share his suite on the train.

Oliver listened to her in silence, his face a study in astonishment. Only when she was finished did he speak. Then he said: 'But you must have been crazy! You mean to say you shared a suite on the train with a man who was a complete stranger! What possessed you, Tona? You of all girls, who would hardly let me touch your hand.'

She did not attempt to argue or defend herself.

'You're quite right, George,' she agreed. 'I probably did go a little mad. I suppose I fell in love with him.'

Oliver gave a mirthless laugh.

'*In love!* And so much for *his* love! The fellow is a damned scoundrel.'

'Perhaps he is,' she said and her head drooped. For she knew that she loved the 'scoundrel,' and must go on loving him all her life.

'We'll soon find out who he is, if he's in Gardenia,' added Oliver in his most pompous voice. 'I'll see he squares up on this business, Tona, you're not fit to look after yourself. That's obvious. You would do well to marry me and let me take care of you.'

She looked away from him.

'Don't ask me to do that, please.'

Oliver, looking at her with resentful eyes, admitted to himself that his feelings towards her could never be purely impersonal. He wanted to comfort her, to alleviate her distress and give her back her pride and assurance, but behind it all was the knowledge that, more than anything else, he wanted to take her in his arms and have her for his own, and that he could willingly murder this fellow, Valentine Carr.

'I suppose you realise what a foolish child you've been?' at length he said.

'Yes,' she nodded, but thought of the tzigane-music and the strange overpowering charm of the man she had loved to her cost.

'Was he English?'

'I don't think so.'

'Anyhow, if he's in this country I'll find him and call him to account. You must want to get even with him.'

His words made Tona wince. Poor old George was no psychologist. There was no question of her wishing to 'get even' with

Val. You did not want to hurt the man you loved, although you might try to forget him and all he stood for.

'I don't suppose I'll ever see him again,' she said quietly.

George lit his pipe and puffed at it noisily.

'You can't want to, either.'

Tona shrugged her shoulders. George was beginning to irritate her (He always had done, at home, at the office, although Kathleen and Tom thought him wonderful. They were always plaguing her to accept his proposal.) Couldn't he realise that the one thing she wanted most was to see Val at this very moment, to hear him speak, to feel the touch of his hand on hers?

She finished her drink and lit another cigarette. In the distance she could hear the deep sound of a bell which had been tolling ever since she arrived at the station. She asked Oliver why it continued to ring.

'It's for the late King,' he told her. 'He died last night. That is why all the public buildings are closed this morning. The old man had a stroke up in the castle. That's the castle over there.'

He pointed towards an imposing grey building standing high on a hill above the town. A flag was flying at half-mast over the battlements. Tona looked at it with aching eyes. The castle was a poem of beauty – a splendid silhouette against the background of tall, purple-blue mountains.

'It's hard to think of death or unhappiness amidst so much beauty,' she said, and suddenly fumbled for her handkerchief and wiped away a tear which trickled down her cheek.

Oliver glanced at her. Slowly he finished his long drink. He scowled at the sight of that tear which Tona had just wiped away. He felt resentful of it and of her whole attitude. He had looked forward to her arrival and expected both to give her a good time and have one himself. It was deplorable that she should have thrown herself into this disgraceful affair with a strange man on the train. And it really was so difficult to imagine Tona doing any such thing. She had always seemed to him a little prude, although never dull or stupid like that sister of hers. He couldn't stand the sister or the brother-in-law, although he appreciated the fact that they were on his side and urging Tona to marry him.

What the devil was it that Tona wanted, he wondered … what had she seen in this fellow on the train … what was there missing in him, George Oliver, that she should not want to throw in her lot with his? Damn it all, he had a good job now and could offer Tona a far better home than she was living in at the present moment.

It annoyed him, too, that Tona did not thank him humbly for his renewed proposal. Not many other fellows, he thought, would have made it after that story that Tona told.

He heard Tona's tired little voice: 'Don't be angry with me, George. I know you are. Perhaps I shouldn't have told you ... but I had to tell someone, it was on my mind, and you've always been so nice to me.'

George set down his glass. That was better. He liked appreciation. He put out a hand and patted hers.

'Poor little thing, you have made an idiot of yourself all right, but I'm not going to judge you.'

'Thank you,' she said under her breath.

He added: 'I don't suppose Kathleen or Tom would be very edified.'

Tona winced at the mere idea of what Kathleen and Tom would say to her.

'I hope they ... will never know.'

George rose and took her arm.

'Oh, well, now then, young lady, I'm going to prescribe a good rest for you. You know it's still early hours. You go up and have a sleep and I'll take the papers down to the office and study them, then I'll call back and we'll lunch together. There's a big café in the Central Square which should interest you. They haven't closed that. They eat well here no matter what happens, and even though the King's lying in state.'

'Was he a good king?' asked Tona, feeling that she must show some vague interest in what George had been telling her.

'Decent old chap. There's always a lot of palaver here. They're crazy about royalty and every other day there is a feast or procession. They're very primitive really, although I believe the King was English in his ideas and has tried to modernise the country. But the people are uneducated and don't take well to alteration of their customs and traditions of centuries.'

Tona stood still a moment. The glare of the sunshine hurt her eyes. The bell from the Cathedral went on tolling. It was a mournful droning sound. It made her want to burst into tears.

She was glad to get away from George and go up to her room and be alone again.

She had been given a big airy bedroom on the first floor with windows leading out on

61

to a balcony. There were brightly coloured mats. The huge bed was covered with an embroidered quilt and the furniture was of some light yellowish wood. There was no water laid on, but the chambermaid – who wore peasant dress and leather sandals and a pointed muslin cap – had just told her that she could get a bath, if she wanted it, just down the corridor.

But Tona did not want a bath, she had already had one in that luxurious suite of Valentine's.

A feeling of deadly depression, of heart-sickness, seized her. She unpacked a few things, the tears dripping down her cheeks.

Then the desire to cry overcame all her efforts. She turned back the embroidered spread, climbed on to the mountainous bed and, flinging herself face downwards, burst into a passion of tears.

She cried herself asleep like a forlorn child. She awakened to hear a knocking on the door and the voice of the chambermaid in broken English saying: 'Mees … Mees … gentleman waiting luncheon.'

'Tell him I'll come,' said Tona.

George had returned for her. Yes, it was half-past one and she must have slept for some hours. Tona slid on to her feet and hastily bathed her face in ice-cold water. Heavens! how her head ached! And back with a rush came the memory of Valentine. Would George find him? Did she *want* him to look for Valentine? Wouldn't it be better if she never saw him again?

She put her hand in the pocket of her coat and drew out the note he had written her. With despairing eyes she read every word again. He begged her not to think too badly of him. He had said that he was 'distraught.' Why distraught? What was there to prevent him from carrying on their affair? Why should he have left her so suddenly and in so cowardly a fashion?

There were no answers to any of these questions. Tona put the letter back in her pocket and hastily combed her hair and made up her face. Whatever she felt, she told herself, she must make more than an ordinary effort to appear normal and even cheerful with George.

She put on a cool linen dress which had a floral design, and a big straw hat, then went downstairs to join George.

'Ah! You're looking more yourself!' he greeted her.

'I'm fine,' she said with forced brightness, then added truthfully, 'and getting hungry.'

For she was young and had a healthy appetite and even grief could not make her lose that appetite for long. Neither could grief render her perpetually unaware of the exciting country to which she had come. So during that lunch in the big café in the Square she tried to give herself up to the pleasure of the moment. A moment which George did not spoil by referring to what she had told him. He could be a jovial host and he set himself out now to please her. He ordered her dishes which were procurable only in this part of the country and Tona found herself eating amazing fish – caught in the mountain streams and cooked with special sauces – and venison which came, he said, from the royal preserves.

The café had a huge striped awning under which they sat protected from the sunlight. Before them lay the lovely Square, flanked by plane trees and timbered buildings.

A fountain stood encircled by a marble basin, around which were hundreds of rose trees in full bloom. On top of this fountain was a winged horse, fashioned of white marble. 'The Winged Horse' was one of the most famous statues in the world, George told Tona, and it had been photographed by thousands of tourists, and was attributed to a famous sculptor of the Renaissance period.

Tona genuinely forgot her troubles when she looked at that exquisite statue; at the delicately raised hooves, the proud nostrils and tossing mane. It was so life-like and so full of strength and poetry, it appealed to her imagination. She thought: 'Valentine would like it ... he would like anything beautiful or artistic.'

And long after she left Gardenia in the days to come, the one thing she remembered most vividly was the Winged Horse and the fountain, and the jets of water spraying the roses. And the smell of roasting venison in this café and all the strange colourful people walking the Square – people who spoke in lowered tones today and hushed their usual singing because their King lay dead.

Towards the end of the meal, when Tona was drinking the best coffee she had ever tasted, she noticed more and more people arriving and lining the streets, and what George called 'musical comedy' policemen in white and green uniforms with cocked hats arrived on horseback and began to direct the traffic. There was a tense air of expectancy which made Tona ask:

'What are they waiting for? What is going to happen?'

'The young King is going to drive through the town to show himself to his people,' he said. 'The porter was just telling me. The boy is very popular with the people. But here we are. You're just in time. Let us go upstairs and see the fun. It should be amusing.'

Tona walked upstairs and out on to the balcony with George, and as she did so a wave of cheering came steadily nearer until it reached a crescendo which seemed to rend the air beneath them. There was a sharp ring of horses' hooves in the Square and the jingling of harness as the head of the procession came into sight. Down below, the crowd were singing the Gardenian National Anthem.

Tona leaned farther over the balustrade. Troops were coming along now, a company of fine-looking men on horseback, their sabres and breastplates glittering in the sun. Behind them she saw a carriage, a quaint, gold carriage which looked strangely in keeping with the picture. In the carriage were two men. The younger, dressed in the uniform of a Gardenian hussar, was bowing from side to side.

A waiter from the hotel rushed out into the street and threw a handful of flowers.

'Valentine!' he cried excitedly. 'Valentine!'

Tona's heart seemed to stand still at the sound of the name.

'What did he say?' she gasped.

A man, standing nearby, answered her in broken English: 'It is our young King, so handsome, so noble!' he said reverently.

Tona gripped the parapet and leaned down to stare at the man in the carriage, and simultaneously the bowing figure turned and the young King looked up at the balcony of the hotel.

Tona found herself looking down upon a face which was stern and brown, with brilliant blue eyes and jet-black hair under the high, strapped hussar's helmet. Did she not know every feature of that face? Had she not kissed those eyes and mouth and traced every line with the kisses he had taught her?

Valentine, King of Gardenia! He was king! Now she understood everything. The scales fell from her eyes and revealed the staggering truth. The man who had held her in his arms and called her his love was a king.

For one timeless moment their eyes met. Valentine of Gardenia saw the lovely, distraught face in the frame of golden hair, the slim, familiar figure. He recognised Tona and stiffened in every limb. His face went white under the bronze. His lips formed her name: 'Tona!'

At the same time he saw her move back into the arms of a man who stood beside her. Valentine moved forward as though to rise, then dropped back in his seat again and went on bowing mechanically from side to side, saluting to the cheering crowd as the royal carriage passed on towards the Cathedral and was lost to view.

4

When Tona recovered consciousness she found herself in her hotel bedroom. The green rush blinds excluded the brilliant sunlight. She sat up quickly and putting a hand to her forehead found it damp. There was a strong odour of *eau-de-Cologne* which suggested that somebody had been bathing her face and had just left her.

Slowly the memory of the last hours began to return to her. Of course, George must have brought her here. She could remember fainting in his arms as the procession passed by. The procession! What a shock it had been! What a shattering revelation! Val, whose arms had held her all through the long hours of that tempestuous night of love, was a king. King of Gardenia.

He was the man who, with his lips throbbing against hers, had said: *'I shall love you for ever...'*

Tona gave an hysterical little laugh which echoed strangely in the silence of her room. Her face was bloodless, her lips twisted with pain. Why had he said that? He must have known all the way along that his love could only endure for a night, and that he must make her look like the plaything of an hour.

King of Gardenia! Could she ever forget Valentine as he had been this afternoon, so stern and handsome and regal, answering the salutes of his people from the royal carriage? He was king of this very country to which she had come. It was intolerable. She did not want to remember that he was a king. She felt no pride, no conceit in the knowledge that her lover was of royal blood. She only wanted to remember that he was a man who had taught her to love him desperately. He had taken – she had given – without reserve. The thing had been too strong for her, but she had believed in him and now...

'I can't bear it,' she whispered, and the fierce pain of wanting him beat back the shame of thinking that he no longer wanted her.

She rose from the bed, where she had been lying fully dressed, and smoothed her crumpled linen dress and began to comb back the damp waves of pale gold hair. She looked in her mirror and the agony in her own eyes frightened her. Was this pale, haunted-looking creature really the Tona Fenton who had lived such a calm and prosaic life in England? Was this the girl who had never known the meaning of love until last night? She looked at the reflection of her slim figure and thought shameful and ecstatically how Val's lips had strayed from white wrist to white shoulder.

Then she thought of George Oliver, fussy, insistent, demanding that she should marry him, and knew that she could not bear to have him near her for long. That night of romance would be the first and last. It was the beginning and the end.

A sudden resolution seized her. She must get away from George, and from this hotel. She could not and would not be beholden to him, and there was no real reason why she should be. Her duties to the firm had finished when she handed over the books and papers which she had brought from England. She was her own mistress now. If she wanted she could wire to the firm her resignation and take a job in Gardenia. There must be work for an English stenographer in the town, and she would find it. In her present frame of mind she felt that anything would be better than being alone with her thoughts. If she found something suitable she would send George a note saying that she had left, and asking him to understand that she was not ungrateful for anything he had done for her.

She pulled her large straw hat over her head, picked up her suitcase and hurried out of the room. To avoid meting George in the public lounge she chose a back staircase and, unnoticed, walked out into the hot sunlight of the streets.

Gardia appeared to be *en fête*. As gay now as it had been funereal for the old king earlier on. Crowds thronged and surged the narrow, winding streets. The rambling white buildings, with their quaint jalousies and brilliant, climbing creepers, were draped with flags. Everywhere was the purple and gold flag of Gardenia, with a gold lion rampant in the centre. The sight of the flags made Tona clench her teeth. These were Val's colours – purple and gold, the colour of the cushions she had pressed under her head while his eager lips had stung the red blood to the whiteness of her throat.

'I must forget him,' she said to herself. 'I must have some pride. God give me pride and help me forget!'

But how could she forget for one moment when his name was shouted from street to street: 'Valentine! Valentine!'

She thought how fickle was the public's fancy when she was caught up and jostled in the merry-making crowds. The old king lay dead, but the young king was more popular and Gardenia had gone crazy with delight after his triumphant procession. There was no sign of the Fascists with whom, George had told her, the country was riddled.

She walked on as quickly as possible until she came finally to a narrower, less crowded street, where her attention was caught by a peach-coloured building with jade shutters and striped awning. The name above the door was *Café Flora*. There were little chairs and tables on the pavement, and through the long windows she saw a gaily painted room which was obviously used for eating and dancing.

Tona was about to cross the road when she suddenly saw a notice with small writing on it. It seemed to be the same notice written in different languages: Gardenian, French, German and English.

'Wanted. A Dancer. Youth and beauty essential.'

She stood staring at it. Then a wild thought seized her. Why should she not apply for the job? She was not a trained dancer, but she had done quite a lot of amateur dancing in London and she knew that she had those invaluable assets of youth and beauty. If they engaged her it would make her independent of everybody, and she could remain in Gardia until she chose to return to England.

Val might have hurt her, but there was a bond between them that nothing could break – a tie of passionate love. Nothing could take that from her. And if she worked at this café she would be near him. Who knew but that the opportunity might arise for them to meet, when she would tell him that she still loved him and that she understood.

She pushed open the swing-doors and walked into the hall of the gaily-coloured café. A tall, thin man with a swarthy skin and a small black beard, wearing a green and purple sash about his waist, and smoking a long cigar, stood by a desk, talking to another man who was writing in a ledger.

Tona seized her courage with both hands and walked straight up to the bearded man.

'Are you the *patron?*' she asked. 'Because I'm English – a dancer – and I want work.'

The man turned slowly, took the cigar from his mouth and looked her up and down. Her heart began to beat fast. She was in the mood not to care, not to mind what she did so long as she could stay in this country and be independent.

With a gesture of proud grace she swept off her hat and shook back her golden hair. The bearded man's eyes narrowed, then he smiled and said in a low, guttural voice: 'Yes. I am the *patron*. So you want to dance in my café?'

'I do.'

'But you are exquisite – English, yes, and a perfect type. Fresh as a rose, yet with the languor of a lily. What is your name?'

She answered recklessly: 'Just – Tona.'

The proprietor turned on his heel and, slapping the other man on the shoulder, pointed to a piano which stood at the far end of the room. He spoke to Tona in broken English: 'I will give you a trial. Dance, Tona! What you will. Shall it be waltz time?'

'Yes,' said Tona.

The man at the piano began to play a haunting gypsy melody with all the fervour in it which she knew was typical of the fierce, romantic people of this country.

Tona never quite knew how she managed to get through that dance, but she concentrated on the lilting rhythm and tried to let

75

herself go. On the tips of her small white shoes, her delicate arms raised above her head, she seemed to float through the air rather than to dance. Her thick lashes hid the anxiety in her eyes. Her red mouth was parted like a sorrowful, opening flower. She danced as fervently as the man played, and the *patron* watched as though entranced, the cigar suspended in his fingers.

When she had finished he gave a shout: 'Bravo! Superb! You are engaged, Tona. At once we make the contract. You begin here immediately – tonight. If you dance for my clients with the same grace, with such abandon and beauty, you will have what money you ask.'

Breathless and hot-cheeked, Tona discussed business with the proprietor, who told her that his name was Max Rosta. She was successful beyond her hopes. He told her that she could live in the apartment over the café with his wife, and that he would pay her a salary of fifty dollars a week, which would be increased if she brought an influx of customers to see her. The Gardenian dollar was worth two shillings. That was five pounds a week. It meant she would easily be able to keep herself and that she would be quite on her own.

Rosta questioned her closely about her private life. He wanted to know exactly who she was, where she came from and why she was here, and she wondered what he would have said if she had told him she had come to Gardenia with Valentine. Travelled here in the arms of a king!

She answered Max as briefly as possible, telling him she had come to visit a friend and that she had quarrelled with him, had lost her money and wanted to be self-supporting for the rest of her stay in Gardia. Rosta saw no reason to doubt this and when she asked if he would send to the hotel for the rest of her luggage so that she need not see George Oliver, or let him know where she was, the man readily agreed.

He gave instructions to a servant about the luggage, and led Tona upstairs to a small, not unattractive flat where he gave her into the care of a stout, middle-aged woman whom he introduced as his wife. Tona found Madame Rosta to be amiable and friendly and able to speak a little English. But Tona was too tired and worn to pay much attention to what the woman said.

After the women had said a few words to each other, Rosta began to issue a string of orders to his wife, who listened to him in silence. She was to get busy at once and make a dress which would be suitable for Tona to wear that evening. It was to be made of flame-coloured chiffon, and she would dance in it and enflame the hearts of his patrons.

'Now I must go and get everything ready,' he said excitedly. 'The Café Flora must look its best tonight.'

A moment later he shut the door of the flat behind him and ran quickly down the stairs to the café, where the man who had played the piano for Tona was once again poring over his ledger.

'Sandor,' Rosta said in his own language, 'this is stupendous luck. This English girl will be worth her weight in gold to us. She will be the perfect decoy. She is innocent and knows nothing, and is as beautiful as a dream.'

The man called Sandor looked doubtful.

'You're sure she knows nothing?'

'Of course I am. How could she?' Rosa lowered his voice and whispered in the other man's ear. 'Tonight when we meet, the others will be told that this girl will help us to seize the throne from the new King, before he has a chance to make his opinions felt. This Tona will be the downfall of Valentine. She will put the State into the hands of the Fascists.'

The pianist shut one eye and smiled knowingly.

'You always have your plans, Max.'

'Yes,' said Rosta, putting a forefinger against his lips and stroking the black, silky moustache, 'I have my plans, but no more of this … until they are ready and the time is ripe.'

Upstairs, Tona sat on the edge of a small high bed (they were all high in this country, with huge quilts and pillows), and watched Madame Rosta put the finishing touches to the little room. The stout, good-tempered wife of the café proprietor was obviously house-proud. She was also quite pleased to let the English *danseuse* occupy this apartment. She brought in fresh linen for the bed, a crocheted spread, which she told Tona, as she chatted volubly, she had made herself and it had taken a year of work, embroidered mats for the dressing-chests and old-fashioned wash stand. A little pottery bowl full of sweet-smelling pink flowers, which Tona saw everywhere in the town, stood on the wide window-sill.

Through the tiny casements framed in fresh sprigged muslin curtains, the sun beat warmly until Madame drew green shutters half across them.

'Too hot for you, eh, Mees?' she smiled. 'No so hot sun in England.'

'No,' said Tona.

But her thoughts were not on the weather, not really here in this little bedroom ... nor with the prospect of her public appearance as a dancer in a strange land. She saw only Val's stern, handsome face looking up at the balcony ... the white flame of recognition that had leapt between them when their eyes met. And she felt that her heart was breaking in two. She wondered what Madame would say if she told her that the new King of Gardenia had broken her heart.

Madame went on fussing.

She had sent Poli, the boy, to fetch 'Mees's' luggage from her hotel she said. 'Mees' must rest now by orders of Monsieur. Food and wine would be sent up to her. Katti, the maid, would bring the tray later. She was a good child, but inclined to be lazy. 'Mees' must scold Katti if she neglected to serve her. And so on, until Tona forced a smile, thanked Madame and told her she needed nothing else.

After Madame's portly figure had vanished Tona took off her dress and lay down. Exhaustion claimed her. Her mind refused to worry further. Everything – even the memory of Val was blotted out.

Tona slept.

So heavy was that slumber that she did not hear her door open. Did not see the figures of Max Rosta and his wife stand there a moment, peering into her dim, flower-scented little room.

Then the door closed again. Outside, Madame Rosta, hands on her hips, regarded her husband with a certain amount of mis-giving.

'Max, you are a mad one always,' she whispered. 'You have plans for the English girl, yes? Dangerous plans.'

'That is my business, Coralie,' answered Max Rosta with a bland smile. 'Yours lies in the kitchen and the linen cupboard, my darling. See that your eyes and ears pry no further.'

She shrugged her huge shoulders, but her dark small eyes looked sullen.

'As you wish, my dearest Max. But I warn you that one day you will go too far. I am afraid for you – for both of us.'

He laughed and patted her back.

'Have no fears for either of us, Coralie. Attend to your house-wifery. Meddling in politics is not the thing for women.'

Madame glanced at the closed door behind which Tona lay so soundly sleeping.

'She is very young, Max. As beautiful as an angel and, I believe, as good. If our child had lived – our little girl whom the angels took from us – she might have resembled the English Mees, with her golden curls and her innocent eyes. Oh, Max...'

'Shut up,' he broke in, his brow darkening. 'Do not mention our child. And leave the English Mees to me.'

Madame Rosta put the corner of her apron to her eyes. She did not understand this strange, fierce husband of hers. Once they had been very happy; content to run a small café in the town and have no truck with rebels or politicians. Those were the good days, she thought sadly – when their one and only child, the little Maxine, had been alive. Since her death – from fever on her fourth birthday – her father had never been the same man. He had grieved for her terribly and begun to drink much and mix suddenly with bad company. Coralie Rosta feared for him. And for herself. But she was afraid to say more. She went down to her kitchen concealing her tears.

5

That night the name TONA appeared in scarlet and gold neon-lit letters above the entrance of the Café Flora.

The stars were not yet glittering over Gardenia's capital when the news began to spread through the town that a new and unknown dancer was to be on view at Rosta's *dancing*. Rosta's cabaret turns were famous. Each night his place was packed with a gay, cosmopolitan crowd. Men of all stations went there to eat and drink and dance – officers of the Gardenian Guards, rich townsmen and foreign visitors. It was unusually clever of Rosta, they thought, to provide a new attraction on this particular night when the town was *en fête*.

Madame Rosta, obeying her husband's orders, had taken good care of their new protégée, encouraging Tona to spend a quiet afternoon and evening in preparation for the night's work. Tona had slept soundly, exhausted by all she had been through. When she woke she was better. She felt fresher and more able to cope with what lay before her. Only when she remembered that she had to dance before an unknown, critical crowd did she experience moments of panic which seized her with the idea of running away and putting it all behind her. But her terror soon passed and she returned to her former state of apathy. What did it matter? What did anything mater now that Val had taken the heart out of her body and crushed it under his careless feet?

Tona lay on the top of her bed watching Madame Rosta and the girl Katti work on the flame-hued dress, without any possible idea that she had taken refuge in the most dangerous place in Gardia. She could not know that the Café Flora was the headquarters of the Fascist element of which George Oliver had spoken to her. She was not to know that the man who had engaged her to dance drew a salary from the Wilhelmstrasse.

Rosta was Valentine's most powerful and dangerous enemy. The Gestapo called him the Gardenian Quisling, knowing that he would be only too glad to become leader of some thousands of anti-royalists who were anxious and willing to turn their country into a Nazi-dominated republic.

Valentine's ascension to the throne was the

moment for which they had been waiting. Already the cunning and insidious propaganda machine was at work. The great mass of the Gardenian people were loyal and content. In which case, Berlin ordered, no effort should be spared to besmirch Valentine's name and reputation. The agents of the Gestapo must sow subtle seeds of discontent, suggesting that the young King had pro-Axis tendencies. During the ensuing days of doubt and discord the Führer would send another army to 'rescue' yet another suppressed minority.

After supper Madame Rosta and a young maid-servant began to prepare Tona for her dance. They massaged her body and rinsed her head with champagne. The wine, which they told her was cheap in this country where it was made, brought out the glossy sheen in the crisp gold waves of her hair. The chiffon dress fitted perfectly, and the women wound silver beads around her throat and thick silver bangles around her delicate wrists. On one slender ankle they clasped an imitation ruby bracelet.

Finally, Madame Rosta touched Tona's little red mouth with a deeper red, darkened the long lashes and skilfully painted blue shadows under her eyes, beneath which worry and anxiety had already left their mark.

It was almost midnight when Tona was called downstairs. There were only soft lights burning on the many supper tables in the café, which was in semi-darkness except for one powerful beam which was directed on her as she took the circular floor. The room was thick with cigar and cigarette smoke and noisy with the clinking of glasses and men's laughter, but there was dead silence once the piano and violins took up their haunting melody and the young girl in her flame-coloured chiffons glided across the floor.

This was the moment for which they had waited. *Tona in the Dance of the Flame!*

After an instant of panic, Tona took part and danced as she had never danced before. She flung herself into the ecstasy of it, and the men and women who watched her were enraptured and fascinated by the youthful grace of the slender limbs and the gestures of her lovely hands and feet.

Rosta's clients had seen many brilliant performances in this room. They had swayed to the rhythmic impulses of the *csárdás* which were as heady as their own Tokay wine, and beaten time to the more modern and sophisticated dancers from the west. But this girl was different. There was a strange magnetic force in her dancing which gripped them. She seemed to have lost all connection with her surroundings. Her eyes were closed as though she were in a trance, only her body moved with the force of the rhythm which was possessing her. She was a flower unfolding before their gaze, an exotic flower which spread its beauty in front of them.

Tona did not seem to care that she was the cynosure of so many eager, appraising eyes. Her mind was burning now with memories of Valentine and of his love. It was as though she danced for him and felt his lips once again upon her mouth and his arms around her shoulders and waist.

When the dance ended the whole room was seething with enthusiasm. This was the most glamorous and welcome spectacle which Rosta had yet given them. *The Dance of the Flame* had been a fitting *finale* to a day which had been charged with excitement.

One handsome young guardsman in the green uniform of his King leaped to his feet as Tona dropped like a tired red flower upon the floor. The women at his table looked jealously towards the girl whose beauty and talent had cast a spell over the room, but they had to admit that she was the best of

Rosta's finds.

'*Mon Dieu!*' cried the soldier. 'I thought English girls were cold, but this one, this Tona, is a living flame!'

Thunderous applause echoed in Tona's ears. One elated Gardenian raised his glass above his head, and after a toast to her smashed it on the floor.

'*Tona!*'

Her name rippled through the room until it grew to a crescendo which was taken up by every voice. Rosta, watching with the inevitable cigar in his mouth, showed his white teeth in a smile of unconcealed pleasure. He had not made a mistake. This girl who had so recently strayed into his life was going to serve a double purpose. She would bring clients and money to the Café Flora and aid the Fascist cause.

It pleased him to think that an Englishwoman might be instrumental in helping to force yet another Balkan country to line up with his German masters. The Gestapo would be quick to recognise his skill. If his plans materialised it'd be the beginning of the end of Gardenia, and the moment for which he had worked and schemed. His ultimate ambition seemed almost within his grasp. Already, in his distorted mind, he could picture the Nazi hordes marching through Gardia's streets, saluting their new Quisling.

He hurried to the edge of the floor and put a hand on Tona's shoulder. By this time most of the people were on their feet shouting for an encore, and Rosta knew that they would have to be treated firmly. It was better management to remove his *pièce de résistance* before there might be any chance of their appetites being sated. There was always tomorrow night and the night after tomorrow. For Tona, he determined, was going to be a fixture until she had served his purpose.

'Do not go on again, Tona,' he said, signalling to the orchestra to strike up a number. 'You have done well. Now you must go to bed. They will come again tomorrow.'

Tona threw a cloak over her shoulders and climbed the stairs to her room. Her cheeks were burning and she was out of breath. Her state of mind was chaotic. She knew that she had been a success. She had only to listen to the applause which followed her up the stairs to realise that her initiation into the cabaret world had been crowned with glory.

How fantastic it all was! What would Kathleen and Tom think? How would the office-staff in London react to the news that Tona Felton had been loved by the King of Gardenia, and was now a dancer in his capital? They wouldn't believe it. Of course they wouldn't. The whole thing was like a colourful dream in which a handsome young man changed a Savile Row suit and Leander tie for the gilded trappings of a Balkan king.

The quietness of her room came as an anti-climax after the tense atmosphere of the café. Tona pushed away the tray of *gulyás* and fruit which Madame Rosta had left for her, contenting herself with a glass of Tokay and a cigarette. She wanted to sleep, but knew that her nerves would not let her.

She walked to the open window and looked over the brightly-lit streets. A bonfire glowed on one of the distant hills, and while she watched a rocket soared into the air to shoot forth a cluster of coloured stars which slowly formed the letter V.

Valentine! How impossible it still was to get away from that name. She could even make out the silhouette of the castle where he was now living. Probably, she thought to herself, he would be attending some State banquet. There would be wine and beautiful women and soft-mouthed courtiers to surround the new King with every worldly distraction. It was foolish to expect him to find time to concentrate on a solitary English girl whom he had befriended in the train.

Tona was wrong.

There were no celebrations that night in Valentine's castle. A few hours earlier, when she was being prepared for her dance, Valentine of Gardenia sat wearily in the oak-panelled library of his apartments, trying to read through an ever-increasing pile of State documents.

It was ten o'clock at night. The tedious ceremonials of the day were over. The castle was quiet and the King was alone – alone with the most bitter and remorseful thoughts of a slim, golden-haired girl – thoughts which precluded his concentrating on any more work that evening.

It had been a trying and exhausting day for Valentine. The dead are buried quickly in Gardenia. After he landed on the airfield on the outskirts of the town he had been driven straight to the castle where his father's funeral rites were about to take place. The long ceremony and funeral oration had wrung Valentine's heart. He had been devoted to his father, yet he was expected to appear in public only a few hours after the gates had closed on the family vault.

That morning and afternoon countless duties and matters of State had to be performed and finally there was the drive through the streets of his capital. It angered and distressed Valentine that he should be expected to act like a heartless automaton. The people were said to love him. Why then should they want him to appear smiling and serene before them when his heart must still be heavy within him? It did not make sense.

The procession through the town imposed a strain on his nerves which reached a shattering climax when he glanced up to see Tona's face looking down at him. For the rest of that day he was to be haunted by the memory of her standing on the balcony. He could never forget her white and agonised face. Who was the man with her – the man whose arms had caught her when she fell? And what must she be thinking of him? Did she remember, as he did, every burning instant of last night?

Valentine's face was pale and strained under its bronze. He tapped nervously on the desk with his pen. He could no longer sit still or pretend to read the papers which lay before him. He must go to that hotel and find her. He had to speak to her again, even though it might be for the last time.

He loved her, and he was tortured by the knowledge that his kingship made it so difficult for him to be with her. His mind was racked by the realisation that it would be impossible for him to marry her.

But see her he must. He was mad with longing for her. A king was only human – only a man. He wanted to lay his head on her shoulder, and, holding her hand, tell her that she was the answer to his dearest dreams. He wanted to tell her about those dreams, in which today's responsibilities were mere soon-to-be-forgotten shadows which faded into a tomorrow where a crown and a throne were displaced by a home and an adored wife.

Valentine rose to his feet and, locking away the pile of documents in his desk, ran up the broad marble staircase which led to the King's sleeping-apartments. A valet hastened forward, but Valentine sent him away with a peremptory dismissal. He did not want the man to see that he was changing into a lounge-suit and soft felt hat, which would be less conspicuous than his uniform.

When he was dressed he pulled the hat well over his eyes, and walked across the castle grounds in the direction of the garages. His long, low sports-car, which he had always driven himself in the old carefree days, was in its usual position. He jumped in and started up the powerful engine. It would take him to the town quickly and would attract less attention than one of the royal saloons.

It was almost eleven o'clock when the Bugatti drew up outside the hotel. For a moment Valentine sat still as though undetermined what to do, then looking quickly up and down the street he swung his legs over the car's low body and walked into the dimly-lit hall where a clerk sat in the reception office.

'You have a Miss Felton staying here,' he said, keeping his face in the shadow. 'I would like to speak to her.'

The clerk answered as he would have replied to any Gardenian gentleman: 'The English lady has left, Excellency.'

Valentine's heart sank.

'She has left!' he repeated incredulously. 'Where has she gone?'

The clerk spread out his hands.

'We don't know, Excellency. She went after lunch. Her luggage was sent for and collected during the afternoon. She left no address.'

'You're sure of that?'

'Quite sure, Excellency. I have no idea where you can find her.'

'Thank you.'

The young King turned slowly away and walked out into the starlight. What did it mean? Why had she left at a moment's notice without leaving any clue to her future plans? Was it possible that she was with the man whose arms had supported her on the balcony? Valentine's eyes narrowed. She had mentioned a man whom she knew in Gardia, some Englishman who had wanted to marry her. He remembered now. She had laughed when he said he was jealous of him. George Oliver. That was the name.

For a moment Valentine toyed with the idea of returning to the hotel and enquiring about Oliver. It was just possible that he might be able to trace Tona through her friend. But what would it avail? It would be kinder to leave her alone. She had said this George was a decent fellow. Perhaps she might decide to marry him and accept the home and security which no King of Gardenia could offer.

Valentine got into the car and, taking off his hat, drew a hand across his eyes. He did not care if he were recognised. At the moment he was oblivious of personal danger, of his kingdom and of his crown. He could think of nothing but Tona, and the knowledge that he was going to pay to the end of his life for the ecstasy which he had tasted in her arms and upon her lips.

His hand was on the starter-switch when a

man hurried towards the car. Valentine turned in his seat and recognised his equerry.

'What do you want, Paul?' he asked wearily.

Paul Lavengro looked anxiously around him.

'I followed you, sire,' he said urgently. 'It is madness for you to be alone and unprotected in the streets tonight. The town is riddled with Fascist agents.'

'You think that worries me?'

'It is your duty to be worried, sire.'

Valentine pointed to the seat beside him.

'Get in, Paul,' he said curtly. 'We'll go home and put you out of your agony.'

Lavengro made no answer. Not until the end of the drive, when the car had been put in the garage and they were walking across the grounds to the castle, did he say: 'You must forget her, Valentine. You must turn your thoughts to your people. Gardenia has need of you. Already there is a spirit of unrest which is being fanned by an insidious propaganda.'

'What of the unrest in my heart?' asked Valentine.

The equerry put an arm around his young King's shoulder.

'My boy,' he said slowly, 'the King of Gardenia cannot be allowed to have a heart.'

6

A week had passed. Tona was now thoroughly at home with the Rostas, and growing used to her life as the star attraction at the Café Flora. She had even grown fond of Coralie, who made a fuss of her. And Max was kind enough.

She worked hard during the day. Rosta had found for her a celebrated local dancing-master who had schooled her in many of the finer details of his profession. Her every gesture had now become one of studied grace and beauty, every lovely movement was calculated to stir the hearts of her audience. Night after night she fascinated them, and she was human enough to be pleased and flattered by her triumphs.

The *maestro* had perfected her. She was no longer a mere talented amateur. She knew that she had it in her power to draw men to her feet. But she wanted none of them. She was impervious to the invitations of the admirers who pursued and flattered her. In a way she felt that she cheated them. She danced like a flame, but her heart was dead within her and she knew that it could only be awakened by Valentine's touch – or by Valentine's kiss.

Tona had spent less than three days at the Café Flora when she determined that she must get in touch with George Oliver. She had been uneasy in her mind about him and her conscience pricked her. George might be irritating and difficult, but he was a good, if demanding, friend and she felt that she had treated him badly.

The least she might do, she decided, was to tell him where she was. He would probably criticise and censure her, but now that she was independent and self-supporting, she could afford to stand up to his arguments. And from a purely self-interested motive it would be a wise course to take.

Her name was becoming a household word in Gardia. It could only be a matter of time before he would hear about Tona, the English dancing-girl, and track her down. Then there might be an unpleasant scene, which was the last thing she wanted to experience. Neither did she want to risk George becoming really worried about her absence and starting an enquiry which might lead to embarrassing complications.

She walked round to the hotel early on a Sunday morning, when she knew that she would be sure of finding him there. The streets were almost deserted, and she kept contrasting the stillness of the town with the noisy crowds which had thronged these pavements on the day when she had set out in search of work without any definite plans and with little hope that anything would materialise.

When she reached the familiar hotel which was so pregnant with memories, Tona ran up the steps and glanced quickly around the empty lounge. There were no servants to be seen, so she crossed to the open french-window and looked across the terrace. It was deserted except for one table at the far end. Tona looked again. That was the corner where he usually sat. Yes, it was George. She could recognise the back of his head and the broad shoulders in the English-cut suit. He was smoking a cigarette. A Penguin novel and a tray with the remains of his breakfast lay on the table in front of him.

She was almost level with him before he heard her footsteps and turned round. For a moment he stared at her as though unable to believe his eyes. Then he stood up and held out a hand. When he spoke his voice was a mixture of anger and relief.

'Tona!' he exclaimed.

'Hello, George,' she said quietly.

'Where the devil have you been? What have you been doing? I've been worried to death about you.'

She sat down on the chair which he pulled out for her, and began to take off her gloves with quick, nervous jerks. The colour had mounted to her cheeks.

'I thought you'd be worried, George. That's why I'm here. I've behaved badly, and I want to try and explain things to you.'

'I certainly think you owe me an explanation,' he said curtly. 'I hardly expected you to walk out without a word. You didn't even leave a note. It's not like you, Tona.'

'It's *not* like me,' she agreed. 'It was rotten of me. But when I left this hotel I was not myself. I was desperate. I didn't want to see anybody I knew, or talk to anyone. I felt I had to get away – I had to do something to take my mind off what had happened?'

'May I ask what you did?'

'I got a job. I've been dancing at the Café Flora.'

An expression of incredulity which changed into one of frank condemnation crossed Oliver's face. Tona knew that she had shattered another of his illusions. This was more than his stolid unimaginative mind could cope with.

'*Dancing!*' he repeated amazedly. '*The Café Flora!*'

She nodded. Under other circumstances his tone of heavy pomposity would have made her want to burst out laughing.

'It's not so bad as it sounds,' she said, forcing back a smile. 'Remember, my mother was a dancer. I've got theatrical blood in my veins. I find it easy to adapt myself to my surroundings.'

'You can hardly compare the theatre as your mother knew it with a second-rate Balkan café.'

'It's very respectable.'

'I hope it is,' he commented dryly. 'How long do you intend to remain there?'

Tona shrugged her shoulders.

'I have no plans. I might leave tomorrow. I'm under no obligation. Don't you understand?' she said earnestly, leaning towards him. 'This will probably be my one and only chance to see the Balkans. I may as well stay here for a bit and try to get something out of my opportunities.'

'You could stay indefinitely as my guest.'

She smiled.

'I know that. You're sweet and generous, George. But it's the last thing I'd do. You know how beastly independent I've always been.'

Oliver turned in his chair so that his eyes would not meet hers. He fumbled with his tie and stared straight in front of him.

'Then why don't you stay permanently – as my wife?' he said jerkily. 'I may censure and condemn your behaviour. I admit I do. Any normal fellow would. But I still happen to love you.'

Tona's eyes misted. She moved forward impulsively and took his hand.

'Dear George,' she said, 'I believe in your love. I value it and thank you for it. But you must admit, I've always been frank with you. I've always told you I couldn't return it.'

Oliver's face was still turned from hers.

'I thought there might be a chance for me now,' he said, without changing expression. 'To be quite candid, I thought I might get you on the rebound.'

'No,' she said firmly, shaking her head, 'I'd never marry a man I didn't love. It wouldn't be fair to either of us.'

He made an impatient gesture as though intolerant of her definite tone, but in his heart he knew it was just some answer such as this that he had been afraid to hear.

'You may change your mind when you forget this other fellow. Have you seen him again?'

'No, and I don't suppose I shall, in spite of the fact that he's here in this town.'

George turned toward her with a gleam of interest in his eyes.

'The devil he is! What is he doing here?'

'He – lives in Gardia.'

Tona was smoking a cigarette and she looked not at George, but at the bluish smoke which drifted from her lips. She could not even *think* of Valentine without a sensation that she was slowly dying, deep down within her.

'Well!' exclaimed George. 'If he lives here, why on earth haven't you seen him and asked him to do the right thing and–'

'He can't marry me if that is what you mean,' interrupted Tona.

There was a short silence. Then George Oliver shrugged his shoulders, which was a nervous habit with him when he was irritated.

'You're off your head, my dear girl.'

'So you've told me once or twice,' she said with a brief smile.

'Well, look here! You know what your sister would say – and old Tom–'

'I know quite well. They'd be horror-stricken and they'd call me every name under the sun and disown me. That doesn't cut any ice with me, George. I think I've grown up a bit since I came out here' – her red lips curved into a faint ironic smile – 'and it doesn't seem to matter what Kathie and Tom think any more.'

He stared at her.

'But you've changed out of all recognition, Tona. I always thought you were, if anything, a little prude.'

She looked at him, the swift colour mounting her cheeks.

'I am in some ways. But I loved that man. I loved him with a force that has astounded myself. He just made me forget the world.'

To one of George Oliver's temperament that sounded like the ravings of a lunatic, or the romantic tripe one saw on films or read in trashy novels. He snorted.

'Stuff and nonsense. You can lose your head for the moment – but you can't go on losing it. You've had a hot affair with this fellow and he ought to marry you.'

Tona gave a set smile.

'I can think of nothing I'd like better. But

it's out of the question.'

'Is he married already?'

She bit her lip. In a vague way she would have liked to have confided in George. But some queer sense of loyalty to Valentine held her back. She could not betray his identity. It was as Valentine Carr that he had become her lover and she must not tell anybody in the world that that man was the crowned King of Gardenia. In any case, she told herself, George wouldn't believe her.

'Dear George,' she said, 'just try to believe me when I tell you that marriage between this man and me is out of the question.'

'Oh well,' said George huffily, 'we'd better drop the subject. Tell me more about this dancing job of yours. You really are a strange creature, Tona. Since when have you handed in your notice to the firm?'

'I sent them a long cable which I couldn't afford,' she told him, 'and explained that circumstances had forced me to resign and that you would communicate with them.'

'That's nice for me. What do I say? That Miss Felton is off her head, dancing at a well-known café and going in for mysterious love affairs and that that news is to be passed on to Miss Felton's relations.'

If Tona hadn't been so unhappy she would

have laughed outright. George was recovering his sense of humour, she thought. Poor, pompous old George – he never had much.

'I deserve your sarcasm,' she said, 'but I must just ask you to try to forgive me. As for the firm and my relations, they can think what they like. I intend to write to Kathie and tell her that I've left the firm and that I am remaining in Gardia, having stepped into our mother's shoes as a professional dancer.'

'Well, it's all very irregular,' he grumbled. 'And what more, you seem to forget there's a war on. This country may be in the thick of it at any moment.'

Tona stiffened to attention and eyed him intently.

'Isn't … King Valentine a friend of ours… England's?'

'Some say he is and some think he's got Nazi sympathies. Most definitely there's a big Fascist organisation in this place.'

'I don't believe the King is unfriendly towards Great Britain,' she said in a low voice.

'No one knows. As far as I can see the policy of the new King is shrouded in mystery.'

She gave a long deep sigh, then glanced at her wrist watch, then sprang to her feet.

'Good heavens, I must go.'

George stood up. He too sighed a little. He wished he were not so permanently in love with this girl. This crazy, beautiful Tona. And he felt a real anxiety about her.

'Keep in touch with me, my dear,' he said. 'It isn't right for you to stay in Gardia and dance at a place like the Café Flora amongst all these foreigners–'

'I'll take care of myself,' she interrupted. 'But, of course, we'll see a lot of each other. You're my greatest friend and terribly long-suffering.'

He smiled in an embarrassed way.

'Well, I'll come and see you dance when I get back from Valega.'

'Where's that? Where are you going?'

'Valega's one of the little neighbouring states where we have a small factory. You ought to know that.'

'Yes, I remember now. It seems to me years and years since I had anything to do with the firm.'

'Well, look after yourself,' he said a trifle heavily.

The next moment she was gone. He stood alone on the terrace, pondering over all that she had told him – definitely troubled.

7

When Tona returned to the Café Flora it was to find the atmosphere charged with excitement. She had no sooner crossed the entrance hall than Rosta ran towards her, followed by his wife, who held a printed card in her hand.

'Tona,' he cried, 'it is good that you are here. I have news for you. Great news.'

She sat down on the edge of the orchestra platform and, taking off her hat, ran a comb through her hair. She felt tired and nervy after the meeting with George, and the revelations he had made about Valentine. She wished that she could have gone straight up to her room, and got away for a few minutes from her temperamental employers.

'What is the news?' she asked, trying to appear interested.

Rosta grabbed the card from his wife's hand.

'There you are,' he said, putting it in Tona's hand, 'see what it says.'

Tona looked at the card. It was of thick

white cardboard with a broad gold border. She handed it back to Rosta.

'It looks interesting. But I can't read your language.'

The *patron* waved his hands in the air.

'But I am a fool!' he exclaimed. 'The news makes me forget. Listen. I tell you what it says. Tonight you are to go to the royal castle…'

Tona jumped to her feet. Her eyes were wide and startled. The blood had drained from her face.

'The castle!' she repeated wildly. 'What do you mean? Tell me.'

'It is a royal command. You are to dance for the new King.'

'For the King…!'

Rosta showed his white teeth in a broad smile.

'Yes, my dear. For King Valentine. Now you understand why we are so gay. This is our final triumph. The Café Flora is made. You are made. Don't you understand?'

'I understand,' she answered, nodding her head, 'but why should he want me? How has he heard about me?'

'That is simple,' said her employer. 'Among my clients is every type of nobleman and aristocrat. Somebody who has seen your performance has told the court officials that you would be worthy of entertaining the King.'

'What time do I go?'

'At midnight,' Rosta told her. He took her arm and patted her shoulder. 'Now you must lie down. There will be much to do this afternoon. You must rest.'

'I think I should,' she said dully. 'I feel rather tired.'

Tona was glad to climb the stairs to the flat and shut herself in her room. She wanted time to arrange her thoughts into some semblance of order. Her emotions were chaotic when she sat down and concentrated on the news. There was the warning which George had given her. It would not be safe for any Englishwoman to be seen with Valentine. But this was different. She was going to the castle in a purely professional capacity. She would have no opportunity to speak to the King, but it meant that she would be able to see him once again before she decided to return to England.

Tonight she would dance the *Dance of the Flame* before the man who had made a living flame of her with his kisses. It would be a fitting climax to her royal romance. She wanted to go. She wanted to show him that she was still holding her head high. She was now the most famous dancer in Gardia, and she would show him what an Englishwoman could accomplish in spite of a broken heart.

For the rest of that day the Rostas discussed nothing but her dancing ... how she would look ... and what she would do. Only when Tona was not present did their conversation take on a sinister, secretive tone. This night was to be an all-important one in the history of Gardenia, and they had chosen Tona, who looked and was so innocent, to carry out their most daring and dangerous plans.

The Fascists, whom Rosta wanted to work up to revolt, were anxious to possess the keys of the royal treasure and the plans of a secret entrance to a subterranean passage which led into the castle. The castle was so closely guarded that it would be impossible for them to make any attack or demonstration against the Court unless they could gain access to the passage, but with the keys, which she would conceal in Tona's handbag.

Rosta discussed the scheme with one of the Court officials who was also in the pay of the Gestapo. It would be simple and foolproof, and there was much more at stake than a mere Fascist rising. The possibilities were limitless.

Madame Rosta was to accompany Tona to the castle to act as her dresser, and during the performance she would be given the keys which she would conceal in Tona's handbag. The Gestapo agent had arranged for Tona to be stopped later in the evening, and arrested for espionage. The result would be a scandal and diplomatic uproar which would hasten Gardenia's entrance into the war on the side of Germany.

Rosta was convinced that if his wife could put the keys in Tona's bag victory would be theirs. He would reach the pinnacle of his dreams, and the fruits of his victory would taste all the sweeter because they had been put within his grasp by his English catspaw.

Half an hour before midnight, when a car arrived to take her to the castle, Tona looked her best, glittering with gems which Rosta had hired for the occasion. She believed him when he told her that she looked as lovely as a red flower in her scarlet dress, and was convinced that she would dance as she had never danced before, although she might be devastated with emotion at the prospect of seeing Valentine again.

As they approached the castle it was to

find it a blaze of light. In the throne-room a thousand lights glittered from great crystal chandeliers and were reflected in a floor of polished mosaic. Around the walls were rich satin draperies in the royal colours of green and purple, and purple flowers massed against green ferns. A brilliant throng of courtiers gathered round the dais where Valentine of Gardenia sat alone on his richly carved chair. The lion-rampant in polished bronze served for a footstool under his feet. His full-dress uniform was white with green and purple facings and gold braid. He looked tired and lethargic, and there was a cynical twist to his handsome mouth which had not been there when he had left Istanbul station, a gay, carefree boy.

When the soft music started and a slim, superbly-dressed girl glided into the centre of the great room, he looked at her at first with a noticeable lack of interest, until suddenly his face flushed scarlet and he moved as though to rise from his chair. His intense blue eyes stared at the delicate white limbs of the dancer, at the pale gold head and the lovely oval face.

'Tona!' he muttered, 'Tona...!'

Nobody heard him. The music drowned his voice. He went as white as his uniform and clenched the arms of his throne. This glamorous dancer in the flowing scarlet dress, this alluring, sophisticated woman whose every posture was calculated to stir a man's heart, was his English love – Tona. It seemed incredible, but it was true.

The first time Tona came past his dais she looked at him for one timeless moment. Their eyes met. There was incredulity in his, pride and dignity in hers – for she could not let him know how she longed to throw herself at the very foot of the throne and say:

'Take me away, Val. Hide me. I'm only for you!'

A wave of amazement burned through Valentine's mind and body. He was excited and profoundly shocked. This English girl whom he had thought so frank and simple, whom he had loved for her shy reserve, and upon whom he had set the seal of his love, was performing like any ordinary dancer from a cabaret. He looked round nervously and saw all the other men in the room watching her every movement. For one wild moment he thought of ordering the dance to stop, but common sense told him that he would have to sit it out to the bitter end. It had been arranged for his amusement, he

114

reflected cynically, this *Dance of the Flame* which was setting Gardia on fire.

'God, how beautiful she is!' he thought. 'How wonderful.'

Now she was poised in front of him on the tips of her toes, the graceful young body swaying to the orchestra's subtle rhythm. Valentine saw those arms and shoulders which he had covered with his kisses in the moonlit carriage of the Balkans Express. He remembered every soft line of them, and the rapture which he had known. It was horrible to think of her dancing here in public in his castle. He could only presume she had fooled him into thinking her *ingénue*. She could never have loved him. Her shyness and reserve in the train must have been a well-rehearsed act such as she was putting on now. Obviously she was hard and egotistical like the other women he had known and forgotten.

The tempo of the music quickened. The dancing figure of the girl was working up to a frenzied finale. The flame-coloured strands of her chiffon dress caressed her body, showing every lovely curve. Valentine put a hand to the high collar of his uniform and jerked it. The muscles of his cheeks twitched and his forehead was wet. This was insupportable. In another moment he would shatter the court and his entourage by leaping from his throne and dragging that seductive figure into his arms.

He would get even with her for this outrage. No! He would kiss her and put an end to the torture, to this consuming longing for her which had never left him for a single hour since their meeting.

Tona went on with the dance until, at the final crashing chords of the wild Gardenian music, she sank down at the foot of the dais, her golden head bowed on her bare white arms. She heard a ripple of applause break over her. 'Tona' had triumphed in the presence of the King. But it was finished. Her little hour of triumph had passed. And what were Valentine's thoughts? She had seen his burning, reproachful eyes fixed upon her, and knew that she had shocked and horrified him. That was understandable. But how could he afford to criticise? Had he not taken her heart and then thrown it aside – this lover who had become a king – this king who could never become her lover?

During the next minutes her reactions were vague and unreal. The first thing she knew was that somebody was placing her cloak around her bare shoulders, and without daring to look back towards the royal party she walked blindly out of the brilliant throne-room to find herself in a long corridor where the floors were of polished marble and the walls glittered with beaten gold leaf.

She stopped for a moment and, shutting her eyes, put the backs of her hands against them. She thought and believed that this was the last time she would look upon Valentine's face. The sooner she left Gardia – the country itself – the better it would be for her. The city held no further promise. She would see George and ask him to arrange her bookings back to London. The hopelessness of the situation brought a moan to her lips, which was suddenly stifled when she felt a heavy hand upon her wrist and heard a voice which said in French: 'You are under arrest.'

Tona raised her head and looked around her blankly. Four men in the uniform of the Gardenian police surrounded her.

'What did you say?'

'You must consider yourself under arrest, Mademoiselle.'

For a moment she was too astounded to answer. Then a nameless fear gripped her and her face whitened. She looked from one man to another.

'What do you mean? What have I done?'

The officer who appeared to be in charge took her bag from under her arm and, opening it, pulled out a flimsy-looking paper and a bunch of keys.

'Here is your answer,' he said grimly. 'You must come with me.'

'But those are not mine. I know nothing about them,' she cried. 'I did not put them there, either. I assure you it's all a mistake.'

'You can tell that to the examining magistrates.'

Tona was too dumbfounded and perplexed to try to understand or make sense of what appeared to be a terrifying drama. She stared at the paper and keys which the officer held in his hand. There had been no mistake there. She had seen him take them out of her bag. But how had they got there? What did it all mean? Trembling and aghast, she managed to ask another question.

'What are you arresting me for?'

The answer came like the crack of a whip. *'Espionage!'*

She leaned heavily against the wall, her eyes dilated with terror.

'But that's impossible. You must be mad. I must…'

She was not allowed to finish her sentence. The cloak was thrown over her shoulders, and she heard the same coldly calculating voice.

'You gambled away your life, Mademoiselle, when you came to the castle tonight. You know what to expect.'

A wave of sheer horror descended upon Tona and enveloped her like a mist which stifled and robbed her of further speech. The next few minutes seemed like an act from a Grand Guignol play. In the terror of the moment she cried out the name of the one man who might help her: *'Val!...'*

Her voice echoed emptily along the length of the corridor. The policemen were adamant in the performance of their duty. They were royalists who had dedicated their lives to the service of the Gardenian royal household, and were incapable of feeling any sympathy for the Englishwoman who, they had been warned, would attempt to betray their young King.

At a word of command from their officer they hurried their prisoner along the corridor, away from the glittering lights and warmth, towards a staircase which led into a chilly darkness lit only by a flickering torch held by a turnkey. Terror-stricken and numbed with the horror of it, Tona realised

119

that she was now in the dungeons of the castle. Smoke from the torch blew against her face. The air was fetid and cold as a tomb.

The police officers pointed towards a small stone cell where there was a single mattress and a stool and one paraffin lamp burning on a high ledge casting fantastic shadows which only served to accentuate the sinister atmosphere.

She said nothing as they pushed her inside and slammed back the door with its little grilled window. She wanted to scream, but fell back in silence when she heard the key turn in the lock. It would be futile to create a scene. There was nobody in this desolate spot who would pay any attention to her, and she would need all her strength to tide her over the next hours.

At length she sank on to the mattress and made an effort to control her nerves. She was ice-cold and shivering but as she grew calmer she began to realise what had happened. It must have been the Rostas who had betrayed her. She had left her bag in Madame Rosta's charge, and it would have been easy for the woman to place those things in it which the police seemed to think were such damning evidence.

'The penalty for spying is death,' the officer had hinted. But that was impossible. It *couldn't* happen to her. It mustn't...

She was still lying on the bed when, some minutes later, she heard the sound of a key in the lock and saw that the heavy iron door was opening. She sprang to her feet, the cloak falling from her shoulders in her hurry, leaving her a strange scarlet figure in the flickering light of the gloomy cell.

Her mind was confused with a dozen different fears. Were they coming for her now? Were they going to execute her in the middle of the night without even the pretence of a trial? Her eyes stared towards the door. A man had entered the cell and was coming towards her. She looked at him wildly. He was a tall, erect figure in a splendid white uniform. Then she knew. It was Val! There was no mistaking that jet-black head and bronzed face. His penetrating blue eyes were burning down into hers.

Tona's voice broke with a muffled sob.

'Val! It's you!'

'Yes, Tona...'

The King of Gardenia stood before her and somehow the sight of him took away most of her feelings of panic and fear. She could feel herself growing strangely calm and self-contained. It was like waking up from a nightmare in which one was about to be thrown over a precipice.

'Thank God you've come,' she cried, putting a hand on his arm. 'Now everything will be all right. For heaven's sake get me out of this place and tell them it was all a mistake.'

Valentine's face was expressionless.

'Was it a mistake?' he asked quietly.

Tona's hand fell to her side. She could feel the blood rushing to her cheeks, and knew that her eyes were filling with tears at the realisation that he doubted her. This was the final blow. Val – the man whom she had loved and idealised – suspected her of plotting against him. That was all he thought of her? She took fire from the idea. All the pain, the anxiety which he had caused her culminated in a sudden longing to hit back. She was trembling in every limb, but she flung back her head and looked him straight in the eyes.

'You believe I am a spy?'

Valentine shrugged his shoulders. The evidence which had been put before him could leave no room for doubt. The little English flower was a myth. What she had done tonight might have cost him his life and his throne. Probably it was her idea of revenge for his treatment of her. An eye for an eye.

'You wanted to hurt me, Tona, was that it?' he said. 'Why don't you tell me the truth. I will understand.'

The laugh which she gave was pure hysteria.

'Of course I did,' she cried, wiping back a tear which trickled down her cheek. 'I wanted revenge, even though it meant betraying your country. I'm glad that I did it. My only regret is that I didn't succeed.'

He clenched his hands. For one breathless moment his eyes took in every detail of the girl whom he had sworn to love for ever. He looked at the delicate white arms, at the perfect little ankles in their dancer's jewelled bracelets. Then he moved quickly towards her and caught her in his arms.

'You don't realise what you're saying, what you're doing, Tona,' he said hoarsely. 'The penalty for spying is death. You don't want to die. You know you don't.'

'What is the alternative?'

'If you plead innocent and stay in this country – I can protect you.'

Her reply was instantaneous and convincing in its sincerity.

'I'll plead innocent, but I won't stay in a country which may be hostile to mine. I'd rather die than live under the "protection" of a man whom I can't trust. For all I know you may be pro-German.'

She did not hear his answer. She could not see the expression which her words brought to his face. All she knew was that she was in his arms. The gold buttons of his uniform were pressing against her body. Now his lips touched hers. He was kissing her mouth and hair and neck. She could feel his warm breath upon her cheeks, and stood rigid and tense, her eyes closed and her arms flung back.

She remembered George Oliver having told her that Valentine's policy was shrouded in mystery. Nothing would induce her to let Valentine know that the wild passion of his embrace might conquer her doubts and resentment, and make her once again the simple girl of the train who had been ready to surrender everything for love.

'Tell me you will let me help you,' said Valentine urgently. 'There's no time to lose. For God's sake say you will stay here. It's your only chance.'

'I refuse to stay in this country!'

'You're mad, Tona. You don't want to die.

You don't want to be shot. You must listen to me...'

'No,' she said, straining back in his arms.

'Hear what I have to say!' A torrent of explanation broke from him. He told her how he had fallen in love with her the first time he had seen her on the platform at Istanbul station. He wanted to show her that his love had burnt up into a flame which had driven everything from his head except the one consuming need of her and the real and sincere wish to take her and hold her for ever. 'I told you you were the only person who counted,' he said tensely. 'I meant it. I would have given all my possessions – my throne and my crown – to have knelt at your feet as a humble lover, knowing I need never part from you...'

'Don't go on,' she interrupted, through clenched teeth. 'There's no point in raking up the past.'

'I didn't meant to hurt you,' he continued vehemently. 'I was unable to tell you who I was. It broke my heart to leave you. I went to the hotel to tell you so. Doesn't that show you that I loved you?'

'Or did you want another glamorous night?'

'Listen to me...'

She shook her head.

'You're wasting your time. Go back to your throne, King Valentine.'

'No, Tona, you shall hear me.' His arms tightened around her, one hand pressing through the scarlet chiffon of her dress against the ivory coolness of her back. 'If words don't matter to you – you shall listen to me this way...'

His lips closed over hers in a kiss which seemed to blot out sanity and reason. How right he was! Words might fail, but this – the throbbing passion of his arms and lips – would finally break down her resistance. He held her close, covering her throat and shoulders with his kisses and burying his face against the golden silk of her hair.

For one terrifying moment she felt herself yielding. One slim arm went around his neck and drew his head towards her. Then she jerked back and twisted out of his arms, wrenched herself free. The door of the cell was unlocked. She pulled it open and ran blindly along the stone passage, only stopping when a group of soldiers barred her way.

'Let me go,' she screamed. 'Let me out...'

An officer put a hand on her arm.

'You must prepare yourself for the end,

Mademoiselle. The court has ordered your execution. There is no need for a trial. Your guilt has been proved.'

Tona broke into a frantic laugh.

'Yes, I'm a spy. I wanted to kill the King. I admit it. I only wish I'd done it.'

She broke off, her mad laughter ending in a sob. The men looked at her coldly. They had no pity for a would-be murderer of their King. She covered her face with her hands. Let them kill her. Let them shoot her down like a dog. What did it matter? Life held nothing more for her. The man she loved, the man to whom she would have dedicated her life, suspected and mistrusted her.

The officer's grip tightened on her arm.

'Come, Mademoiselle.'

'I'll come,' she cried, looking from one soldier to another. 'Take me away and shoot me. End it quickly – that's all I ask.'

She looked over her shoulder to see if Valentine were behind her, but there was no sign of him. He was not following her or preventing these men taking her away. There was no sound in the dark subterranean passage except the muffled tread of marching feet. Now she found herself being led up a long spiral staircase. Somebody had put her cloak about her bare shoulders, and a moment later she was in a courtyard at the back of the castle. She stared blankly in front of her. She was so dazed with suffering that she was not astonished to see that dawn was breaking. She had danced late into the night. But she would never dance again. A jagged streak of orange cut across the darkness of the sky. When she looked back she could see the castle, its frowning battlements silhouetted against low clouds which grew lighter with every moment.

A cool wind blew across her face and suddenly, shivering from head to foot, she was seized with panic. She had asked, hysterically, to die. But she didn't want to die. She wanted to live.

In front of her a line of soldiers, each man carrying a rifle, was standing to attention. The firing squad! A wave of sheer terror gripped her. What had she done? She had chosen to die, to be riddled with bullets, to be hurled into eternity. She had chosen it rather than be helped by a man who might use her against her country.

The officer who was now guiding her to a position against the wall eyed her curiously. He thought he would always be haunted by the classic beauty of that pale young face and by the youthful figure in the shimmering silver cloak which looked so strangely garish in the grey light of the dawn.

Tona wanted to cry out. To say: 'Stop! Send for the King. Don't murder me. I'm too young to die. I love life too well!'

She hung on to her courage desperately. She would show these foreigners how an English girl should die. White to the lips, she faced the squad and tilted back her golden head. The officer was tying a silk handkerchief around her eyes. The dawn breeze lifted the pale curls which hung about her brow. Was all this really happening to her? Was it really Tona Felton who stood on the threshold of death? She could no longer see. And soon there would be darkness and oblivion, and never again would she watch that marvellous sun shine down upon a marvellous world.

She gave a little moan and swayed unsteadily at the sound of an order which rang sharply through the crisp air. She knew it must be the order to fire and felt thankful that she could not understand the language. Her whole body was tense and rigid. She waited, but death did not come hideously as she had expected. Instead she felt two warm hands grip her wrists and untie them, and a moment later she realised that she was being lifted bodily into a man's arms and carried away from that grim wall and out of the courtyard.

Tona tore the handkerchief from her face and rubbed her eyes as the first slanting ray of sunshine touched her face. A soldier was carrying her across the castle grounds towards a private road where a black saloon car with drawn blinds stood waiting. She was too bewildered to concentrate on the sequence of events in which she was involved. She only knew that she was unutterably thankful to be still alive and to feel the warm sun against her cold body. Behind her she saw the highest turrets of the castle gleaming like living gold in the glory of the sunrise. She had had her first experience of a Balkan castle and she prayed that it would be her last.

When she was put inside the car she just had time to see a dark handsome man who climbed in beside the chauffeur. He was the leader of the firing party. The man who had prepared her for death. But why was she not to die? What accounted for this last minute change of plans? There was only one possible answer. It must be something to do with Valentine. She felt certain that only the King could have countermanded the order for her execution.

There followed a long and tedious journey over twisting and bumpy roads during which Tona could see nothing through the curtained windows of the car. She lay back against the cushions and stretched her weary limbs. The reaction of the last hours left her physically and mentally exhausted. She was too tired to think or worry about what the future might hold in store for her. The present was all that seemed to matter. She was alive and uninjured and felt incapable of dealing with any further horrors.

Only when the drive came to an end and she found herself being taken into a small white house with red shutters, which seemed to be built in the heart of a straggling green forest, did she evoke any interest in her surroundings. The officer showed her into a small room, exquisitely furnished and bearing every sign of comfort, where, for the first time, she began to question him rapidly and breathlessly. But her flow of questions remained unanswered. The man only shrugged his shoulders to show that he did not understand, and smiling gravely pointed to a table which was spread with a cold meal.

Tona shook her head impatiently. She was much too agitated and perturbed to think of eating. The only thing she did want was to know why her life had been spared and where she was now.

The man did not relieve her curiosity. His behaviour showed that he was anxious to get away, and a moment later, having clicked his heels and saluted her, he locked the door of the house behind him and hurried towards the car which had been waiting, the engine turning over.

Tona ran to the window and looked out. There was nothing to see save an impenetrable curtain of trees in the rich gloom of the mighty forest. A strange silence brooded over everything, and she realised with dismay that she was alone in the house. She was a prisoner. But whose prisoner, and why she was held captive, she could not fathom.

She sat down in a chair and put her head between her hands. She did not want to rest, but sheer exhaustion soon overcame her and at the end of a few minutes she lay back and fell into a heavy sleep.

It was several hours later when she awoke to hear the sound of a car's tyres on the gravel drive which led to the house. Tona sprang to her feet, alert and prepared for any emergency. The engine was switched off, a door was slammed and now footsteps were approaching the house. She looked towards the front door. Somebody was turning the key in the lock. Then the door swung open and she was astonished to see the familiar figure and bearded face of the proprietor of the Café Flora.

'*Rosta!*' she exclaimed.

He came up to her, his eyes flashing excitedly.

'My little Tona! So you are alive and well. They have not hurt you. How thankful I am!'

She looked suspiciously into his narrow beady eyes and smiled coldly. When she spoke her voice was hard and challenging.

'No, they didn't hurt me. They merely threw me into a cell and then put me in front of a firing-squad.'

'I know that,' he said urgently. 'I found out what they did to you and where they brought you. Thank heaven you are all right.'

She gave a bitter laugh.

'You didn't seem so anxious about my health when you sent me to dance before the King. You must have known my life was in danger. Your wife was the only person who could have put those things in my bag. What do you have to say about that?'

'Come, Tona,' he said, spreading out his hands, 'you will not reproach me when you learn the truth.'

'What do you mean?'

He seated himself on the arm of a chair and took a cigar from a leather case in his pocket.

'You may think I should have told you this before,' he began. 'But I did not dare to confide in you until you had proved yourself. Now I know I can trust you. You have refused to pander to this young fool who is on the throne.'

Tona could not hide her astonishment.

'How do you know that?' she asked incredulously.

Rosta smiled complacently. He was convinced that the story he was about to tell her was a masterpiece of complicity.

'You look surprised! I do not wonder. But you see, I know everything which goes on in this country. That is why I'm employed by the British Intelligence Service…'

She swung round on her heel.

'The Intelligence Service!' she repeated slowly. 'You mean you are a British Agent? You work for us…?'

He nodded.

'Exactly. Listen, Tona. You did well last night. During the disturbance I managed to lay my hands on a lot of useful things –

including the keys of this house.'

'This house,' she broke in, breathing hard and fast. 'What kind of a place is it?'

'A royal shooting-box in a forest famous for its game preserves.'

'Then it was Valentine who sent me here?'

'Of course it was,' Rosta continued. 'Don't you see, my dear, how useful you can be? You captured the hearts of the people with your dancing. Now you have captured the heart of this new king. It is he who gave orders for your life to be spared. You have been released for his pleasure. He intends to come to you here – tonight.'

Tona stared at Rosta, her eyes dilating. A wave of hot colour scorched her face. So that was it. There seemed no reason for her to doubt her employer's word. It was quite obvious that Tona, the dancer, was to be detained for His Majesty's pleasure in one of the royal country residences. But she would not stay here. She would escape Valentine at all costs. He was mad if he thought he would find her here tonight ready to sink into his arms. He had saved her life. Well, that life was her own – not his. After this final humiliation she would go to any length to evade him.

'Do you intend to take me away now?' she asked.

'That is why I came here.'

'Then why don't we go?'

'We'll go now,' he said, moving towards the door. 'There is plenty of work for you to do. Come quickly before we are overtaken. With my wits and your beauty, we will settle King Valentine.'

Tona laughed a little wildly.

'Very well. I'll do your work. But wait – I want to leave a note.'

'Nothing incriminating,' he warned her.

'You can rely on me,' she said evenly. 'We're both on the same side now.'

She found a pencil on a desk in the far corner of the room and wrote hastily on the back of an envelope:

'When you read this you'll know I have gone. Perhaps you will now believe that I prefer death to dishonour. – T.'

Rosta watched her fold over the envelope and, addressing it to Valentine of Gardenia, place it in a prominent position on the mantelpiece. Then with a last look around the room she picked up her cloak and walked in silence towards the waiting car.

8

Later that afternoon Tona lay on a sofa in the Rostas' flat, enjoying the luxury of complete relaxation. It was really rather wonderful to be back at the café and to feel that the nightmare of the previous night was over. She had been persuaded to take a good lunch of food and wine, after which the curtains in her room had been drawn and she had slept soundly for two or three hours.

The Rostas made a great fuss of her, anticipating her every wish. From now on she was to be their most potent ally and they realised that it would pay them to spoil and pamper her. After tea Madame Rosta sat at the foot of the sofa and began to massage her ankles.

'Tonight you will dance for us again,' she murmured soothingly. 'Once again these little feet will twinkle over the floor.'

Tona nodded. Her bare white arms were behind her head. Her eyes were half closed. She felt in a queer exultant mood. She had

137

been very near to death. But that had not made a coward of her. It had given her courage. A fierce courage which she hoped would make her really useful to the man whom she believed was working for the British Government.

She was becoming more and more convinced that Valentine was a potential menace to her country. Oliver had hinted at it, and now Rosta assured her that the young King was a ruthless despot – a man who cared only for women and wine and who was willing to neglect his people. She would never remember that shooting-box in the forest without a flush of indignation staining her cheeks. To be taken there and to await his pleasure. How dared he!

However dear the memory of that night in the Balkans Express might be, however much she might love him still, it could make no difference. She would not – she must not – allow herself to remember that love. Valentine had hurt her irreparably, but more important than her personal feelings was the fact that he might be working against her country.

Her flow of thought was interrupted when Rosta burst into the room, the usual cigar between his full red lips. Madame Rosta continued with the massage and Tona, lifting a mirror from the table beside her, examined her face and finding it pale and strained began to colour her cheeks and lips and darken her long curled lashes.

Rosta was the first to speak.

'Tona,' he said excitedly, standing by the head of the sofa, 'I have a wonderful plan. I have come from a meeting with our friends. We have formed a scheme in which only you can help us. If you succeed it will be a triumph.'

Tona, touching her nose with powder, looked towards him with sudden interest.

'What is it you want me to do?'

'I will tell you.'

Drawing up a chair, Rosta began to speak in a low, confidential voice. One practised lie after another fell from his lips to form a convincing story. He told the credulous Tona that the Café Flora was the headquarters of the Fascists who believed him to be one of their most ardent supporters. Already the secret police had searched the premises without finding anything which could deliver him up to the law. He was playing the Fascists' game in order to get information for Whitehall. It was dangerous work, but he assured her that he was willing to run any risk to help the Allied cause.

During the last few nights a certain Baron Nicholas had been coming to the café. The baron was a general in Valentine's army. A brilliant soldier and politician, he was known to have a weakness for a pretty woman, and it was common gossip that, some time ago, he had been entranced by the beauty of Tona, the dancer.

Rosta became even more explicit. If they could get the baron into their power much could be achieved. Nicholas knew every movement and thought of the military party, and Tona was obviously the one to lure those secrets from him.

'Here is my plan,' the *patron* continued. 'Tonight when he comes here you will make yourself singularly charming to him. After the dance you will allow him to take supper with you in a private room. It will be easy to put something in his wine which will loosen his tongue. When he becomes communicative you will ask him the questions which I will tabulate for you.'

'What am I to find out?'

Rosta smiled.

'The Fascists wish to discover exactly how an entrance can be obtained into the castle. When that is a *fait accompli* they can overthrow the troops and make a demonstration in the castle itself. During the ensuing disorder I will try to obtain some papers which are vital to us.'

Tona listened with quickening pulses as Rosta enlarged on the scheme. She realised it was a big thing which he was asking her to attempt. It was a dangerous game to play, but she could manage it. She felt certain that she could deal with the baron in a satisfactory manner and extract the information which Rosta required. But what about the consequences of her act? How would it affect Valentine? It might conceivably mean the end of the monarchy.

Rosta saw her put a hand to her eyes and shudder. He guessed what was passing through her mind and leaned towards her.

'You must not let the personal element come into this. Remember it is your duty.'

Tona sat up, her eyes blazing. Rosta might have discovered Valentine's feelings for her, but she would never let anyone know that she had loved the King. That was her own secret which she would take to the grave.

'I will do what you say,' she answered tersely. 'Give me my orders and they will be carried out.'

It took Rosta less than half an hour to

explain the details of the plot, and for the rest of the afternoon and early evening Tona was able to rest and prepare for the work which lay before her. By night she felt fit and confident, and when she ran on to the ballroom floor it seemed to the clients of the Café Flora that the *Dance of the Flame* was performed with even more abandon than usual, with a wilder grace and more feverish intensity. They found her dazzling and alluring from the pale gold head to the small swiftly-moving feet.

Tonight she wore a purple chiffon dress, tight to the hips and flaring down to the ground. Her slim ivory legs gleamed through the transparent material. There was a jewelled girdle about her waist and purple stones, bunched like glittering grapes, over both ears.

Baron Nicholas had been pointed out to her. Tonight he was sitting alone at a secluded table at the far end of the room, but she felt that his eyes never left her and knew that he was watching her every movement.

'Poor fool,' she thought. 'He will be easy.'

When her dance was over and the café was ringing with wild applause, Rosta, very much the beaming *patron,* led Tona to the famous soldier's table and introduced her.

142

Tona looked at him curiously. He was a magnificent figure of a man, this Baron Nicholas, but spoilt from her point of view by dark horn-rimmed spectacles, a black flowing beard and heavy moustache. He wore smart undress uniform with decorations. A short military cape was thrown over the back of his chair.

He took the hand she gave him and brushed it with his lips.

'Superb, Mademoiselle!' he said in a deep husky voice. 'An exquisite performance.'

'It is kind of you to say so.'

'Never have I seen such dancing. It sets one's heart on fire. Will you honour me by taking supper with me?'

'It is I who am honoured, Baron.'

The soldier jumped to his feet and picked up his cloak.

'In that case we will go now. Is everything ready, Rosta?'

'Everything is prepared, Excellency.'

Rosta bowed and led them from the smoke-laden atmosphere of the ballroom into a small private room where a table had already been set for supper. French windows opened into the garden. A wild, beautiful garden flooded with moonlight. Tona refused to look at the beauty of the night.

Such beauty hurt too much, and she did not want to be hurt or remember love, which was so akin to beauty. She only wanted to be cool and detached and to accomplish what she had set out to do without a single feeling of remorse.

The Baron was an amusing and polished conversationalist. During supper he entertained his guest with an easy flow of amusing anecdotes. His manners were impeccable. Only when their meal was finished and the waiter had left the room did he take her hand and begin to pour out a torrent of admiration.

Tona sat back in her chair, looking at him from beneath her heavily-painted lashes. Her lips were hard and cynical. The baron was obviously under the impression that she was flattered by his attentions. He was reciting all the stereotyped lies which she knew he must have told to countless other women by whom he had been attracted. His blatant insincerity almost pleased her, for never again could she believe in any man's love. All her life she would recoil from any serious affairs of the heart.

She kept reflecting on the futility and artificiality of the present situation. The baron was making himself cheap and fatuous.

Here was a clever soldier, a trusted servant of the King, cutting a ridiculous figure in front of one of Rosta's dancing girls. When he attempted to take her in his arms she shook her head and placed a soft hand over his lips.

'Not yet, Baron,' she told him. 'You work too fast. I like more subtlety. Let us have another drink.'

Nicholas gripped her bare arm.

'Loveliness, I would rather die than frighten you. Shall we drink to each other – to the possibilities of love?'

She nodded.

'That would be charming.'

He leaned across the table to fill their glasses with champagne, and Tona dug her nails into the palms of her hands. This was the moment for which she had been waiting. She must act quickly and surely. Raising herself on the tips of her toes, she smiled into his eyes. The baron did not hesitate. The next second he had caught her in his arms, crushing his mouth against hers. Tona made a supreme effort. His face was still pressed against her hair when she dropped the powder which Rosta had given her into the soldier's glass. An instant later he released her.

'Now I will drink to your beauty,' he exclaimed. 'Then we will walk in the garden. You will look bewitching in the moonlight. See how the stars have come out to adorn you.'

The baron's face was flushed, his voice excited and triumphant, but not until Tona walked away from him did his expression change. Then the eyes behind the heavy spectacles became brilliant and alert. With a quick jerk of the wrist he threw the contents of his glass into a flowerpot, but when Tona turned back to him the delicate glass was raised to his lips as though he had just drained the wine.

'I'm ready,' she said, putting her cloak over her shoulder.

'Then we will go.'

He slipped an arm through hers and led her down a short flight of steps which led directly into the garden. From the distance came the gay lilt of a Gardenian waltz played by the Café Flora's orchestra. The air was rich and fragrant with the scent of syringa.

Tona congratulated herself on the first part of her work. Everything had gone without a hitch. The baron had taken the drug. Now she need only wait until it took effect. Her suspense was short-lived. They had hardly reached the lawn before she saw him stagger and put a hand to his head.

'What the devil is the matter with me?' he said thickly. 'I feel dizzy. I believe I'm going to faint.'

Her heart leaped. Rosta had been right. The drug was almost instantaneous in its effect. Now she must lead him back to the room and persuade him to talk. But first of all she must give the signal which would tell Rosta that everything was going according to plan. Taking a small electric torch from the pocket of her cloak, she flashed it three times in the direction of the café.

The torch was still in her hand when she saw that the little garden had filled with men. Tona looked around her fearfully. The peaceful atmosphere of the flower-filled lawn had become impregnated with impending danger. She did not need to look twice to see that the figures who surrounded them were not Fascists. They were soldiers in the distinctive uniform of the Royal Regiment of Guards. This was the end. Her career as a British Agent had been of short duration.

She gave a little cry and looked around her wildly. The moonlight played upon her, the purple gems flashing against her ears. Her ivory limbs were like statues through the transparent chiffon of her dress. Once again her lips formed a cry, but this time she made no sound. A cloth was flung over her head and for a moment her heart seemed to stop beating.

It was with a desperate effort that she tried to control herself and remember what Rosta had instructed her to do if she found herself in any emergency. On the fourth finger of her right hand she wore a large emerald ring which one of the Café's wealthiest clients had asked her to accept. She had worn it as a mascot. Now she just had time to slide it from her finger and let it fall silently to the ground. Rosta and his men would search the garden and when they found the gem glittering in the moonlight would know to follow her.

A moment later she felt herself being carried from the garden, and when at last the cloth was removed from her eyes it was to find herself back in the private room where she had so recently supped with the baron. She was lying on a sofa, and Nicholas, his arms folded across his chest, stood looking down at her.

Tona sat up and pushed her damp hair

back from her forehead. She was determined that she would not be the first to speak. Anything she could say would be sure to incriminate her, and it would obviously be to her advantage to learn what attitude the baron intended to adopt. His first words told her that he had full knowledge of the plot in which he was to have been the victim.

'The tables are turned, Mademoiselle,' he said curtly. 'You are the one who is going to do the talking.'

There was a short pause before she answered, during which she tried to collect her thoughts into some semblance of order. When she did speak her voice was unconvincing and confused.

'I don't know what you mean,' she replied feebly.

'Perhaps this will help you to understand.'

The baron leaned towards her. No longer was he the slow-moving, placid soldier. With a quick movement of his hand he pulled away his beard and spectacles. Tona stared at him with unbelieving eyes, her heart beating wildly. The transformation was sudden and complete. The man who stood there gazing down at her with a thin, cynical smile on his lips was Valentine of Gardenia. It seemed incredible, but it was true. The baron had

149

been Valentine in disguise. It had been a clever disguise and a brilliant piece of acting. Even she, who had loved him and laid in his arms, had not guessed his identity.

Tona tried to talk, to question him, but she could do no more than murmur his name.

'*Valentine!*'

'Yes,' he said, looking straight into her eyes, 'I only hope this will be a lesson to you. You should stick to dancing, my dear. It's more in your line than espionage. You're not safe to be entrusted with dangerous drugs. You might have given me a nasty headache.'

'I didn't intend to hurt you,' she said involuntarily.

He laughed harshly.

'Don't ask me to believe the impossible. You meant to drug my general and extract information from him which would give me into the hands of my enemies. I suppose you admit that?'

'I admit nothing.'

'Very well,' he said, with a shrug of his broad shoulders. 'What you admit or don't admit is really immaterial. You are a spy. You did your best. I admire you for that, but you would have done better to have stayed in my shooting-box and met me there.'

'Why do you say that?'

He sat down beside her and put a hand on her bare shoulder. His face and movements were calm and controlled, but his eyes blazed in the brown face which she had once thought the most handsome face in the world.

'I was in a mood to be tender and forgiving then,' he said slowly. 'Now I am not.'

Tona braced herself against the back of the sofa and tried to push him away from her.

'Why should you be the one to speak of forgiveness?' she half cried. 'You have only yourself to blame. You brought this trouble on yourself.'

'You suggest that *I* am to blame because *you* are a spy?'

'You drove me to it. You told me you loved me – and I gave you everything. What you didn't tell me was that you were a traitor to your country – and to mine.'

His eyes narrowed dangerously.

'I advise you to keep politics out of this discussion.'

She threw back her head with a proud gesture.

'Can't you stand the truth, King Valentine? Does it hurt you to be called the Gardenian Quisling? Are you ashamed of your friends in Berlin and Rome?'

Tona saw that her words and the contempt in her voice had struck home. His face coloured and for a moment she thought he had lost control of his temper. Then he rose to his feet, making an obvious effort to hold himself in check. When he spoke his voice sounded almost normal.

'In your country,' he said, 'a man is held to be innocent until he is proved guilty. Isn't that so?'

'It is.'

'Then you should try to remember it. Don't give credence to a story until you are sure of your facts.'

Tona was silent. This was a situation which she had never anticipated. Oliver had told of his suspicions regarding Valentine, and Rosta had confirmed them. But neither of the men had furnished any concrete evidence that the King was working for the enemy. There was no apparent reason why she should suspect Rosta of distorting the truth, but the more she thought about it the more obvious it became that she had nothing positive with which she could charge Valentine. The thought that this man who had been her lover, and whom she had loved, might really be innocent of plotting against her country, flashed through her brain. She tried to dismiss it as dangerous and wishful thinking, but his last words had germinated a seed of doubt in her mind which was not to be instantly eradicated.

She was about to question him more closely when a sudden noise from the direction of the garden made her forget everything else. There was a sound of running footsteps, the hoarse shouting of men, and finally the unmistakable crack of a revolver shot.

Tona sprang to her feet and began to run towards the long window, but Valentine was there before her and pushed her back towards the centre of the room.

'What is it?' she cried. 'What's happening?'

He did not answer until he had retraced his footsteps and stood beside her.

'Merely that I seem to have counted myself the victor too soon,' he said with a calmness which amazed her. 'Once again you hold the trump cards. My men are outnumbered. Your godless crew appear to be in charge of the situation.'

She put a hand to her throat.

'You mean the Fascists…?'

Valentine nodded.

'Yes,' he said with an ironic laugh, 'this is

your big chance, my dear. My fate appears to be settled. If I go outside this room I will probably be shot on sight. All you need do now is to give the alarm. Tell them that the man who is with you is – the King.'

The noise in the garden was increasing and Tona's eyes widened with nameless fear when she heard the shouting of the mob outside rising to a crescendo. She could hear voices calling the baron's name and knew that the Fascists would soon break into the café and search every room for their prey.

'What can we do?' she whispered.

The King shrugged his shoulders as though waiting for her to come to some decision. She had never admired him more than now when he stood there, apparently unperturbed, a disdainful smile curving his lips, the handsome dark head flung back arrogantly.

'I've told you what to do,' he repeated. 'Tell them you have somebody here – a man whom they want more than they want poor old Nicholas. What are you waiting for?'

It was his bravery and courage in the face of the danger that threatened him which decided Tona. Rosta had told her that she must not let the personal element enter into her work, but she would not surrender Valentine until she had heard from his own lips that he was hostile to her country, or until she had been given some infallible proof of his pro-German tendencies. She could not betray this man who had been her lover as long as there was the slightest shred of doubt. A deep-rooted love of fair play made her suddenly hate the shouting crowd which swarmed outside demanding the blood of this man.

Once her mind was made up Tona acted quickly. Running across the room, she picked up his disguise and pushed the heavy spectacles and beard into his hands.

'Stay here' she panted. 'I'll see what I can do.'

She did not wait for his answer, but hurried out of the french windows and shut them behind her. She forgot that she was half-naked, that she had had no time to put on her cloak, but she did not feel the keenness of the night wind which curled her flimsy skirt against her slim body.

At this moment when she stood alone facing the leaders of the Fascists she made a strangely beautiful and barbaric figure, her jewellery flashing in the moonlight. She was determined to keep them at bay, and when she saw the familiar figure of Rosta approaching her, steeled herself for the effort. His appearance did little to reassure her. There was a revolver in his hand, and he looked white and angry and totally changed from the suave, affable proprietor of the Café Flora.

'We saw your sign and then found the ring,' he told her urgently. 'Nicholas must have smelt a rat, but we soon fixed his men. You have done well. Now we have only to get him.'

Tona thought desperately, racking her brains for some story which would help her to play for time.

'Listen, Rosta,' she said, putting a hand on his arm. 'That would be madness. To murder Nicholas would merely be to rouse the anger of the whole royalist party. It would not help us. It's information you want. Let him go – for the time being, anyhow. I will see him again. He's crazy about me. I know I can make him talk.'

It was the first plausible argument which had entered her head, but she did not falter, persuading him to let the baron go in peace and assuring him that it would be to their ultimate advantage.

At first Rosta seemed unwilling to believe

that she could deal successfully with Nicholas even though she had time and opportunity, but in the end she could see that he was weakening in his original resolve which was to burst open the windows behind her. Finally he turned to harangue the crowd, and she could guess from the violent discussion which followed that he had been advising them against an immediate attack on their enemy.

Her supposition proved to be correct.

'You're probably right,' Rosta told her grudgingly. 'The fellow is more use to us alive than dead. You can arrange another meeting with him some other time. I've no doubt you can persuade him that you knew nothing about the attempt to drug him. It all depends on your skill – and loyalty.'

'You can count on my loyalty.'

Tona meant what she said. She had every intention of remaining loyal to Rosta. After all, he represented her country's interest which must always be her first concern, and if she found that Valentine was in any way impeding that duty she would stop at nothing. But until she had the proof of his culpability in her hands she could not – and would not – let them murder him.

Rosta's influence and oratory had swayed

the Fascist crowd who were now gradually retreating across the lawn, muttering among themselves. For some minutes he stood at the top of the steps watching them, and not until the last figure had disappeared into the darkness did he pocket his revolver and turn towards the room behind him.

The *patron*, like his dancer, had been doing some hard thinking. His natural instinct had been to lead the crowd into the café and spill some of the hated loyalist blood. But he was astute enough to know that the baron's death would be a minor incident compared with the main project which he had in view. It would also mean the end of Tona's assistance. She would realise that he had been acting the part of a British Agent, and her day of usefulness would be over. He had no alternative but to follow her advice and assumed the role of the friendly proprietor, anxious to serve and protect his famous client.

When Rosta finally pushed open the french windows and entered the softly-lit supper room, his ingratiating explanation for the baron was already prepared. But the words died on his lips. One glance was enough to tell him that there would be no need for any conversation The room was silent and empty. The baron had gone.

Tona looked over his shoulder, half-thankful and half-afraid. Then she heard his deep, guttural voice: 'So our bird has flown while we were settling his destiny! Through that window, I suppose.'

Tona looked in the direction which he indicated and saw a small open window which gave over a courtyard. A curious light came into her eyes. Valentine had certainly outwitted his enemies. While they had been clamouring outside for his blood, he had coolly made his escape into the darkness.

She paid little attention to Rosta's grumbling, but as she passed back into the café, wrapping her cloak around her, a little sob of sheer exhaustion tore her throat. She was deadly tired. It had been a feverish, stormy night, and under the mask of paint and powder, the exotic mask of Tona the dancer, there was an ordinary girl – a girl who had loved madly and given everything for love's sake.

She knew now quite undeniably that she wanted her lover back again. She wanted to feel his arms around her – to escape from the strange, wild nightmare of the life which she was leading, and experience once more that heavenly dream of passion which she had shared with him.

Alone in her bedroom, burning tears filled the beautiful eyes which enflamed the hearts of the men who came to watch her dance. She was too exhausted to remove her make-up with her usual care, and the pale, soft young cheeks were still smudged with black from the mascaraed lashes when she flung herself upon the bed.

Morning found her strangely depressed and heavy-hearted. It was not that she expected Valentine to communicate with her. Yet she would have liked to have heard from him. Their last meeting had been such a stormy one. It broke her heart to know that there was enmity between them. But she had to mask the pain of her thoughts and guard her secret concern. There was no alternative. Already it seemed to her that Rosta was watching her more closely, that his wife eyed her curiously and that neither of them was quite so confidential or intimate.

She tried to comfort herself with the thought that it was a mere flight of imagination, that there was nothing to worry about. But at the same time she realised that she must be more than ever on her guard. She could not afford to make the slightest slip. It would be fatal for them to entertain any suspicion that she had cheated the Fascists and kept the hounds back when they were so near to the kill.

The rest of the day was spent as usual, resting and reading and idling away the hot, sunny hours until it was once again time for her work. She was bathed and perfumed and massaged by Madame Rosta's skilful fingers. Her golden hair was brushed and combed until it rippled like glittering silk, and when the woman was finished with her the exquisite body was smooth as ivory and white as the marble bath in which she had lain.

During the morning and afternoon she saw little of Rosta, but he told her that he would be coming to see her alone that night after her dance.

'We must discuss your visit to the baron,' he said. 'There is much to talk about concerning our future plans.'

Tona, lying at ease on a sofa, smoking a cigarette and fondling a beautiful Maltese cat which had been given to her as a mascot by one of her admirers, flashed Rosta one of her most disarming smiles and told him she would do exactly as he wished.

Only when he had gone did she shut her eyes and continue to stroke the animal's soft fur with her long, sensitive fingers.

'You have sharp claws under your velvet paws, Mircha,' she whispered to the purring cat. 'And so have I, and I will use them to defend my country – and perhaps the man I love.'

The next moment she was having to fight against tears because she had lost Valentine. She was conscious of an unbearable loneliness. Valentine was a king. He was utterly removed from her. But worst of all was the realisation that she did not know if she could trust him.

Her train of thought was broken by the entry of one of Madame Rosta's maids, who came to her with a letter. Tona took it indifferently. Letters were constantly reaching her from admirers – men who had been enthralled by her beauty and dancing and who sought a meeting with her. But when she opened this one and scanned the few lines her languor disappeared. Her cheeks grew scarlet. She felt suffocated with emotion. It was a message from the King. *From Valentine*. Only too well did she know that firm, legible writing. Only too often had she read that note which he had left for her in the train after their unforgettable night.

This one said:

'Tona, I must see you. It is vitally necessary. There are things which you and I must say to each other. You must come. When your dance is finished tonight drive to the Silver Stork. Ask for Mr Kurt. I will be waiting for you. –V.'

Tona read the letter twice. Every nerve in her body was quivering. Her eyelids closed. A dozen wild thoughts swam through her excited brain. He wanted to see her. He had said that she *must* come. She felt instinctively that, although the letter was worded cautiously, it was the summons of love. He did not want to fight or hurt her. Of that she was convinced. It was the Valentine of the Balkans Express who demanded her presence.

For the remainder of the evening she was radiant, buoyed up with repressed excitement. She never danced more divinely, nor gained wilder applause, although her mind was far from the terpsichorean triumph.

Rosta had been fairly easily dealt with, showing little surprise when she told him that she was going out with one of his richest clients, and that she would be ready to receive her orders on her return. Now there was nothing to do but hope that the time would pass quickly. She literally lived for the moment when she could get a carriage and drive through the starlit night to the Silver Stork, which she knew to be a little inn on the fringe of the castle grounds.

Only for one fleeting moment did some of her old resentment against Valentine flare up, and she thought: 'I will not go at his bidding. I will not.'

But the next instant she knew that she must, that her heart would not permit her to do anything else, that if she died tomorrow she must, first of all, hear that beloved voice and feel the arms of her lover around her once again.

9

The young King of Gardenia, under the name of Mr Kurt, waited for his guest in a private room of the Silver Stork. It was not a particularly luxurious room, but it had been converted into a bower of flowers. The flowers had come from the castle gardens. Great dewy masses of roses, carnations and lilies filled the air with their scent and glorified the ancient inn with their beauty.

A deep, cushioned sofa was drawn up before a crackling log fire which the landlord had lit to warm and please his guests. A small table was set for two on which an exquisitely cooked cold supper had been laid. A bottle of champagne stood ready iced in a silver bucket.

Valentine paced impatiently up and down the polished oak floor, smoking one cigarette after another. He looked curiously English tonight, in his perfectly-cut dinner jacket and soft white shirt and collar.

The landlord's wife had found their unknown visitor amazingly handsome.

'A man,' as she told her husband, 'whom any woman could adore.'

But there was only one woman whose adoration Valentine wanted, and he was tormented with anxiety lest she did not come – in case she had decided to punish him by staying away.

Not until the moment when he heard a light knock on the door did he cease his restless pacing and spring to attention. Then in answer to his call, a slim figure wearing a dark hood and cloak hurried into the room. His heart gave a wild leap. The girl's face was hidden in the shadow, but he knew instantly that it was she. Tona had come.

She closed the door quietly behind her and stood leaning against it as though out of breath. Through the closely-drawn hood her eyes met his, and her own heart seemed to be on fire at the sight of him. Here was the lover of the Balkans Express. No longer was he King of Gardenia – but king only of her heart and body.

He moved to her side and took her hands, pressing them with his strong warm fingers.

'Tona – my very dear...'

She answered him brokenly.

'Val!'

'You've come to me.'

'Yes.'

'And you know why I sent for you?'

She was trembling violently, but her eyes never left his face.

'No – I don't.'

'To thank you,' he said. 'To tell you how grateful I am to you for having saved my life, or at least helping me to escape. I got through that window while you were talking to Rosta. Why did you do it? I wronged you. Why didn't you take your revenge when you could?'

'Because I found it – impossible.'

'Because you still love me?'

'Don't ask me that.'

'It could only be because you still love me,' he said, pushing back the hood from her face with eager fingers.

'I can't answer you, Val.'

The touch of his fingers intoxicated her, and she could see that he was like a man drunk with joy at the sight of her face. He unfastened her cloak with shaking hands. It dropped from her shoulders and he saw that she was wearing the same dress in which she had danced when he last saw her. She stood beside him in all the witchery of her perfect womanhood. She did not reply to his question, but in her half-shut eyes and parted lips he read all the signs of passion, and felt that he was answered.

Every nerve in him throbbed. Every vein seemed on fire, until finally his control broke down and he seized her in his arms to crush her lips with a kiss which seemed to be the beginning and end of his world.

'Tona,' he murmured, 'My own dear Tona. How long is it since we kissed like that? Too long. I love you. I can't lose you. We can't go on fighting each other. Do you still think of that night – our night – on the train? Do you? Answer me...'

She was conquered and she knew it. She no longer wanted to resist. She did not care what had happened in the past, nor what the future held. She was only conscious of the sweet temptation of the moment, of the old delirium which swept through her body while she lay against his heart and felt her lips open like a flower under the fierceness of his kiss.

Her arms went around his neck and pulled the dark, splendid head against her golden one.

'You must know that I remember. How could I ever forget? It was madness – but it was heaven.'

'A heaven we shall find again,' he whispered. 'There has never been another woman like you, nor ever can be.'

Tona sat down on the sofa and allowed him to talk. His words thrilled her. He told her that they must start again; that he had been cruel to her, ruthless and thoughtless in his passion. But he had learned his lesson. Now he knew that there could be no life without her by his side. He was willing to give up his kingdom – to abdicate. It had been done before and it could be done again. He would renounce all rights to the throne and throw away his crown, in order to become her slave.

'You can't do that, Val,' she said, shaking her head. 'Too much is at stake. Too much depends on you at this moment when your country is ringed round with enemies.'

'Gardenia has better brains than mine,' he answered impatiently. 'At best, I'm merely a figurehead. If I could help my country, nothing would induce me to leave.'

She drew a deep breath, for a moment her eyes looked into his, and she read sincerity in them – and desire which was as absolute as it was fierce.

'Val, my dear,' she said soothingly, her fingers threading through his thick, dark hair, 'don't say anything tonight which you may

169

regret. Just remember that I love you, and that I'm here with you now – in your arms.'

His lips strayed to her white throat where a pulse beat madly for love of him, and he held her so closely that he could feel the wild throbbing of her heart. Then their love seemed to blend them together, until it exalted itself in broken sighs and still longer, deeper kisses.

'There can be no alternative,' he said at last. 'You must marry me. You must be my wife.'

'Your wife!' She repeated the words slowly. 'You know that's impossible, my dear.'

'I tell you it's *not*, Tona. I will abdicate at the first opportune moment. You and I will go away together to some place where we can shape a destiny for ourselves. Then we will find our own happiness.'

'My darling Val,' she said, touching his warm brown cheek with her hand, 'please believe me when I say that I love you. I love you desperately, even more than I did on the train. But I'm a woman – and I'm afraid.'

'Of what?'

'That if you gave up so much for me, there might come a day when your love would cool, and you'd regret it. I couldn't bear that…'

He cupped her face in his hands, and as he looked into her misty eyes his heart seemed to melt within him.

'Don't speak of regrets,' he answered gravely. 'The dearness, the loveliness of you means more to me than life itself. I'm laying that life at your feet – your little white dancing feet. Can you deny me? Can you refuse to be my wife?'

Tona tried to regain some vestige of control. She knew that his words were genuine. He was a supreme lover, the lover of her every dream, and he was hers for the taking. But she must be convinced of his loyalty – not to her but to her country.

'I don't want to deny you anything, Val,' she said seriously. 'You must know that. But we haven't only ourselves to think about. We have the interests of our respective countries to consider. If we neglected duty or loyalty, our happiness together would be a travesty – a mockery.'

He shrugged his shoulders.

'I agree with you. But I've already said that my abdication would not affect Gardenia.'

'*But it might affect Great Britain and her Allies.*'

Valentine jumped to his feet and stood with his back to the great open fireplace.

His face was an expressionless mask. Only a nervous twitching of his mouth suggested that he had been troubled by her words. She had spoken slowly and deliberately and he had not missed her implication. It was obvious that her principal worry was not that his love might cool and cause him to regret his abdication. She doubted his loyalty to England. That was the real cause of her apparent anxiety.

'Tona,' he said, after a short pause. 'I am a king. A servant of my country. I have sworn allegiance to that country, and until I am formally released from my obligations there must be matters of State and policy which I cannot discuss – even with you.'

'I realise that,' she said, rising to stand beside him. 'I don't want to know any State secrets. I only want to know what *you* feel. I'm entitled to know my own lover's thoughts.'

He put a hand on her shoulder and turned her towards him so that he could look into her eyes.

'I know you are a British agent, Tona,' he said evenly, 'and I know that you are working for love of your country. That is wholly admirable. It pleases me – because I also love your country.'

'You mean that, Val?'

He nodded.

'I swear it. It is your lover who is speaking now, not the King of Gardenia. At the moment I can't give you any proof of my loyalty to the Allies. I can only ask you to trust me. But I may trust nobody. Not even Nicholas himself. Lately I have had reason even to doubt *him*.'

Valentine's words and the solemn sincerity of his voice brought a lump to Tona's throat. She found it impossible to believe that he was telling anything but the truth. When he spoke there had been a light in his eyes which could only have been the light of truth. She was convinced of his loyalty and integrity, and the conviction removed the only insurmountable barrier to her personal happiness.

'I do trust you,' she said ardently, 'and I can't deny you. If you want me I will marry you.'

Now she was back in his arms again. He laid her gently on the sofa opposite the leaping fire and put a cushion behind her head. Then he knelt beside her, pressing her hands to his lips.

'My own lovely one,' he said. 'Tomorrow I will send you a message telling you where to meet me. There will be a priest. I can arrange it. You will belong to me for ever.'

She answered him with a kiss, her white arms pulling him down to her. For a moment there was silence. His head rested on the cushion beside her. Their lips and arms were locked in one breathless embrace after another.

Suddenly Tona started violently and sat up. Was it her imagination, or had she seen a face at the window? An evil, watching face? The blood turned to ice in her veins. She sprang from her lover's arms and stood rigid and tense. Supposing Rosta had followed her. Supposing someone had seen her here with Val, and heard what they said. She knew only too well the penalty which the Fascists would mete out to a traitor. If they suspected her of treachery it would be the end.

'What was that?' she said fearfully.

Valentine was at her side.

'What do you mean, darling? What are you talking about?'

Tona made an effort to calm herself. Probably her eyes had been playing tricks with her. She was stupid – giving way to nerves at the very moment when her happiness was so near at hand. She smiled bravely.

'It's nothing, my dear. The wind blew the curtains across the window. It gave me a fright. Hold me close, darling. I love you so. I'll come when you want me. I will be waiting for you – living for the hour.'

Valentine laughed excitedly. He crossed to the table and poured out a glass of champagne, held it to her lips and made her drink, then drained the glass and smashed it in a thousand pieces on the floor.

'That is the Gardenian symbol of marriage,' he said, taking her in his arms, 'already you belong to me. You are mine, my own beloved Tona. My own lovely flower whose beauty and fragrance I will guard for the rest of my life.'

10

The rose and opal of the dawn was already breaking when Tona left the Silver Stork and hurried back to the Café Flora through the sleeping town of Gardia.

She walked as though on winged footsteps, her body and brain still intoxicated by the sweetness of her reunion with Valentine, her thoughts dwelling on his last words when he had put on her cloak and arranged her hood about her face.

'This may be a disguise for other men,' he had said, 'but I would know those eyes and lips if you wore a thousand masks. If I were blind, and you touched me, I would know that it was you and no other woman in the world.'

Alone with her burning memories, Tona did not know that the shadowy figure of a man slunk furtively after her, stopping when she stopped, or moving quickly into the shelter of an open doorway if she turned to look behind her. The shadow did not disappear until she let herself into the café, where a yawning waiter, sleepily clearing up the debris from the night's festivities, handed her a note.

The note was from Rosta. It was curt and to the point, telling her that he must postpone their meeting until the next night, as she had left it too late for their discussion.

Tona felt a little uneasy as she climbed the narrow staircase and sought her bedroom. Did Rosta suspect anything, or was it merely her guilty conscience? Certainly, she would have to see him and spin some tale which would allay any doubt which might be dormant in his mind. She felt thankful that it would only be a matter of hours before Val would send for her, and she would be able to turn her back on this fantastic life in the café.

The anticipation of that next meeting with the man she loved soon banished every other thought from her head. She undressed hastily, and, stretching her arms luxuriously above her head, fell into a deep sleep from which she did not wake until late in the morning.

When she opened her eyes it was to find her room flooded with sunshine. Tona sat up excitedly. It was wonderful to think that before that sun set she would be with Val.

He had promised to send word to her at the first possible opportunity. At any moment now there might be a knock on the door, and she would receive the message.

Every time her thoughts dwelt on the prospect of their future marriage, the blood coursed through her veins. The knowledge that Val was a king, willing to renounce a crown for her sake, was thrilling enough in all conscience. But it seemed little to her compared with the realisation that he was just a man who loved her and who had chosen her for his wife.

All that day she carried on bravely with the dancer's usual routine of rest and massage, but she chafed inwardly against every indolent hour which passed. Each time Madame Rosta's little maid entered her room she sprang up with beaming eye and kindling heart. Was this the message from her lover? Surely it must come soon!

As the day slipped by and the sun set and darkness fell swiftly over the city, all Tona's excitement and joyous anticipation died away. Her heart beat slowly with anxious dread. Her cheeks were pale under the rouge, and an uncontrollable fit of restlessness seized her. She paced up and down the room, careless of the fact that Madame Rosta eyed her inquisitively, and oblivious of a set, dangerous smile which curled the bearded lips of Rosta himself.

Why didn't Valentine send for her? He had given her his word, saying that he would arrange for the secret ceremony soon after sundown. But now the stars were out in all their glory, and from Valentine there was nothing save an ominous silence.

For the rest of that evening every moment was a secret torment. She was bewildered, afraid, and completely at a loss about the whole affair. Valentine had broken his promise. He had not sent for her. Surely he could have got some sort of message through to her! *He had promised!*

He could not mean to hurt her like this at the eleventh hour.

It was with the greatest difficulty that Tona performed her dance that night in the Café Flora. She danced badly. She knew it. And although her beauty still entranced Rosta's clients, her movements had lost their wild grace and abandon. Twice she got out of time with the music. It was impossible to concentrate on her work when she was only conscious that her heart was wrung with pain for the lover who had failed her.

When the dance ended she realised that

the moment had come when she must face Rosta to discuss his future plans, and she wondered if she could act her part without giving herself away. Every thought, every nerve and emotion was centred on Valentine. She felt that in another moment she would forsake common sense and pride, and rush through the night to the castle to demand an audience with the King, and find out for herself what had happened to him.

She was utterly distraught when she went up to the Rostas' flat after her last performance in the café, and stood for a moment at the window of her bedroom looking down at the narrow, picturesque street. She felt exhausted by her emotions and fears, and was still lost in her reflections when the warm silence of the Balkan night was broken by the sound of trumpets; a clear clarion call which echoed across the roof-tops. Almost immediately it was followed by the strains of music, the rhythmic tramp of marching feet and the ring of horses' hooves on the cobbled streets.

Surprised and interested, Tona threw her cloak over her shoulders and stepped on to the balcony. In the distance she could just see the red glow of torch-lights illuminating a long procession of soldiers, and as they grew nearer she realised that these men were the Imperial Guard of Gardenia. Their brilliant uniforms were lit up by the torches carried by men who ran along on either side of the street, and following the mounted guard came a white saloon car in which two uniformed men were sitting.

Tona stared down incredulously. She could not fail to recognise the younger of the men. How well she knew every line of that figure, that dark, handsome head and the strong, aristocratic profile! It was Valentine! The King of Gardenia was passing in a royal procession under her very window.

The music blared out. A cheering crowd ran wildly after the car. Tona could hear their voices shouting: *'Avido! Avido!'*

It was one of the few Gardenian words which she knew. It meant 'good-bye.' She felt suddenly crazed with a nameless terror and leaned far out over the balcony.

'Val!' she called. 'Val…!'

The King did not look up. He did not even glance in the direction of the Café Flora, but continued to sit stiffly upright in the car looking stern and weary, saluting the cheering crowd mechanically.

The procession passed on until it was out

of sight, and Tona fell back, an icy chill gripping her body. What was happening? What did it all mean? The people were shouting *'Avido'* – farewell. Valentine must be going away. But where? And why? What was the reason for this midnight journey? Why hadn't he told her or sent some message? It was incredible. At this time last night she had been lying in his arms while his straining arms, his passionate lips had told her a thousand times that he worshipped her, body and soul.

She crouched back, her hands shaking. She felt utterly bewildered and utterly miserable. Then she heard a low, mocking laugh and turned to see Rosta standing in the room, his hands locked behind his back.

'You watch the procession, eh, my dear?' he said, eyeing her closely. 'It is good, eh? Our King goes to Valega to fetch his royal bride.'

Tona stared at him, her heart giving a wild leap, and when she spoke her voice was shrill – almost hysterical.

'You're crazy, Rosta,' she cried. 'You don't know what you're saying!'

Rosta gave a deprecating shrug of his shoulders.

'I'm merely repeating what everybody

knows,' he said slowly. 'Valentine will travel all night and be with his fiancée by the morning. He will stay as a guest at the castle of her father, the Prince of Valega. It is good diplomacy. Gardenia would welcome an alliance with the Valegas. They are wealthy, and our Government needs money to balance the budget. They say the young Princess is very beautiful...'

'It's a lie!' Tona cried. 'You're inventing the whole story.'

Rosta thrust his face closer to Tona's. He could see for himself that the face of the beautiful dancer was a white suffering mask.

'The news disturbs you,' he said, his eyes narrowing. 'But what can the royal marriage mean to my little dancer?'

Tona lost her last vestige of control. Clutching her throat, she ran across the room towards the door.

'It can't be true,' she gasped. 'He can't be going away to this woman!'

It was the cry of a tortured heart, and more than enough to confirm any suspicions which Rosta might have been fostering during the last few days.

'So!' he said menacingly. 'It is true. You think you are in love with this king. You are on intimate terms with him. You were a spy in my pay, and at the same time you were Valentine's mistress. Don't deny it. I know everything. I no longer wish to employ you. You are beautiful and popular – have made much money for me – but you have also deceived me and betrayed our cause. Now you must be punished, my dear.'

Tona shrank against the wall. So it was true. Rosta was obviously telling the truth. Valentine had gone – to contract a royal marriage. He who had sworn last night, promised against her lips to make her his wife, had done this infamous thing to her. He had lied. She had sacrificed everything for a man who neither loved her nor wanted her. He had just played with her, toyed with her for an hour, for that one night, before throwing her aside. It was the story of the Balkans Express all over again. For one night's madness she had been betrayed a second time.

When she finally glanced towards Rosta, the sinister look in his eyes struck terror in her heart, and drove even the thought of Valentine from her mind. Something seemed to freeze in her heart.

'What are you going to do with me?' she asked quietly.

'The penalty of treachery is death,' answered Rosta. 'You know that, don't you?'

Tona pressed both her hands against her throbbing temples. It was the second time she had heard that awful threat. She thought: 'I want to die. I'd rather die, now that *he* has gone to another woman.'

Rosta put a hand on her arm and swung her towards him. He was smiling again, a hard calculating smile.

'Don't alarm yourself unnecessarily,' he said evenly. 'I think you are too young, too lovely for death. Another punishment will be more suitable. There is a fine old fortress close to the frontier. It is a prison for people who we think are safer out of this country. It will do admirably for you. You will have plenty of time there for meditation.'

Tona clung to his shoulder.

'No, please. I'd rather die than be imprisoned for life. Let me die. I *want* to die!'

Rosta pushed her aside and turned to leave the room.

'I dare say you do,' he said smiling coldly. 'But I happen to wish otherwise. There are different ways in which a beautiful woman can help me. You will leave here tonight under escort, my little dancing spy.'

11

Tona looked at Rosta in a stupefied way.

'I leave – tonight! No, I don't believe it. You can't do this to me.'

Her knees seemed to give way beneath her and she sank to the floor and crouched there, the pale gold hair tumbling about her fevered eyes.

For a moment she closed those burning eyes as though to shut out the picture of Rosta's evil face. When she opened them again he was gone and she was alone.

There was no sound in the room, but from the distance she could still hear the tramping of feet and the dim music of the Imperial Guard who were escorting their king to the station.

A low moan broke from her lips as she collapsed and lay with her face hidden against her bare arm. She knew now infinitely she wanted to die. Death would be a welcome release from the agony of misery which consumed her. For the second time Valentine had betrayed her. For the second time love, which had seemed so sweet, had become such a bitter thing that it was intolerable.

The words of a poem by Heine, which she used to sing at home in London, filtered through her mind.

'Twice have I loved unhappily.
Twice has love passed me by.
Oh, Sun and Moon and Stars laugh on,
I laugh with you and die.'

Tona knew that never again could she go through such an agony of humiliation and futile longing for a man whose arms and lips had claimed her with breathless passion. A man who forgot her when his desire was satisfied.

But she wasn't to be allowed to die. That was too quick – too merciful. She was to be kept in a grim fortress, sentenced as a traitor, condemned to unbearable hours of remembering – and regretting – until she would surely go mad.

'I can't bear it,' she whispered, and her body, slim and lovely through the purple mist of her dress, was shaken with wild weeping. She loathed Valentine. She loved him. She could kill him for the suffering he had caused her, yet she would give her life to have him back. But if ever she saw him again she would show him what he had done to her. She would prove that he had turned her from a woman who could love into one who could hate. Never again would her arms curve about his neck and her lips thrill to his kisses. That was finished for ever. He was going to another woman – to the young Princess of the Valegas. Well, let him go! But one day he should pay, one day *he,* in his turn, would be punished.

During the next few hours Tona remained in such a stupor of misery, in such a dazed condition of body and mind, that she hardly knew what was happening to her. The room seemed to fill with people, the Rostas predominating. Madame Rosta, no longer a kind friend to flatter, to console her, but an enemy – scared, suspicious, regarding her as a spy; and Rosta himself, cold, sinister, threatening; men who were in his employ, men disinterested in the English girl's beauty – concerned only with their political intrigues and difficulties.

Tona realised that it would be futile to attempt an escape, and equally futile to raise her voice and cry for help. Who would hear her in the small hours of the morning in a Balkan town? Only too often had she heard a cry ring through those streets, where violent passions, hates and desires followed swiftly on the jewelled heels of glamour.

At her husband's order Madame Rosta took away her flimsy evening dress and jewels, and helped her into some plain dark travelling clothes. She put a heavy coat over the girl's shoulders and tied a scarf around her head. She was warned that if she made any resistance it would merely increase her punishment at the conclusion of her journey. Good behaviour, Rosta added, might warrant a certain amount of leniency.

Tona felt that she must be playing a part in some fantastic nightmare when at length she was bundled out of the café toward a waiting car. Real horror seized her – dread of the unknown fate awaiting her. As she stepped into the car she looked up to see the sky ablaze with stars.

'Perhaps I will never see them again,' she thought. 'Perhaps I am about to die. But it doesn't matter. Nothing matters now that I have lost Valentine for ever.'

She saw no more of the Rostas that night. The three men who accompanied her were loyal Fascists, disinterested in her as a woman, contemptuous of her because they thought she had betrayed their cause. When she spoke to them they made no answer. They ignored her and talked swiftly among themselves in their own language.

Tona soon gave up appealing to them. She concentrated on her thoughts. She tried to forget Valentine, but her imagination was too vivid to allow this. She kept picturing him, the gay, handsome young king talking in his own enchanting way to the young princess whom he meant to make his queen. So well did Tona know that he was a king of lovers. She could imagine how the princess would respond to his every word and glance. She had seen a photograph of the girl – Julia was her name. Princess Julia of Valega. Tall, dark, handsome, with a reputation for riding magnificently, like a boy – for shooting – hunting – a young 'Diana,' able to join in the royal sports with the sports-loving King of Gardenia.

A suitable wife, no doubt, but would Valentine really love Julia of Valega – as he had loved *her*, Tona? Had he not sworn he liked small, slender, fair-haired women – the feminine type like herself?

Tona clenched her hands until the nails dug into her palms, but she did not notice the physical pain. Her mental anguish submerged everything. The drive seemed interminable. She went on torturing herself with thoughts of Valentine and Julia together. It was many hours later that she found herself being led between the men on to the platform of a small out-of-the-way railway station, where a train stood waiting. The men led her to a compartment which had apparently been reserved for them. A minute later a bell rang, a whistle blew and the train began to move.

Tona sat back in her corner like one numbed with fatigue and misery. She was sick and cold. Her throat was dry and she had a craving for a drink and for sleep. Nobody offered her any refreshment, and in spite of her deadly fatigue she was too miserable to sleep. About an hour later, when the train was speeding through wild, moonlit country, one of the men in her carriage looked at his watch and spoke to her for the first time. They were over the frontier, he said in faltering English, and would shortly reach the village which was their destination.

Tona had opened her mouth to reply when the accident happened. Her most vivid recollection was of a sickening tearing crash. The lights in the carriage went out. There was the sound of smashing glass and splintering wood. Sounds which were soon mingled with the screams of the terrified travellers trapped in the debris.

Later she was to find out that it had been a head-on collision with a goods train. A signalman's mistake. Carriages were telescoped and flung in wild confusion across the line. Two of the men in her carriage were killed instantly and the third seriously injured. It was only by a miracle that Tona herself was not killed.

When she was dragged from the train by a rescue party, the express had just crossed the frontier into the neighbouring state of Valega. But the people who rushed to the scene of the accident from the nearest hamlet neither knew nor cared who Tona was or why she was on the train. The kind-hearted peasants were merely concerned with her physical condition. Her left arm was badly cut and one of the women busied herself in bathing and binding up the wound.

At first Tona was conscious only of a human and overwhelming relief at her escape from death. She sat quietly on a rug on the grass, too dazed and shocked to think very clearly. Then it flashed through her mind that she was alone. Her guards seemed to have disappeared – they were dead or dying perhaps. Here was her chance of escape altogether from Rosta and his Fascist satellites. Her arm throbbed and her head ached, but the thought of freedom stimulated her to action. She rose unsteadily to her feet, and without further hesitation began to walk quickly away from the railway track.

In the midst of the confusion which followed the accident nobody noticed her departure, and she soon found herself on a rough hilly road. She had no idea where the road would lead her, but it ran in the opposite direction from which she had come, which was all that seemed to matter.

The accident had taken place just before dawn. Now it was morning. A gloriously warm sun shone down from a cloudless sky. Tona looked dazedly around her and saw that she was surrounded by beautiful wooded country. The birds were singing. Close by ran a stream, crystal clear, gushing from the rocks. It was all like heaven after the hell of the night. Suddenly, utterly worn out, she collapsed, lay down on the grass. She slept. It was the sleep of sheer exhaustion and she did not wake until noon.

She was roused by the distant sound of a car. Rubbing her drowsy eyes she stood up and stretched her aching arm. She looked sleepily down the road. A large saloon car was coming towards her, a green and silver car which flung up a cloud of white dust.

'Perhaps they will give me a lift,' she thought hopefully. 'I must try to make them understand that I'm English and that I want to be taken to the English Consul.'

She moved into the centre of the road and waved her hand at the oncoming car. It stopped close to her. Tona saw two women were sitting in the back seat. One was young and very attractive, with raven black hair, bright brown eyes and a warm olive skin. She was dressed in pale green and long green feathers curled round the brim of her small chic hat. She wore a rich brown ermine cape over her shoulders and looked altogether in striking contrast to her companion, who was elderly, even dowdy, dressed in sombre clothes and appeared to be a servant rather than her companion.

The younger of the two gazed in frank astonishment at the girl who stood in the road. Tona presented a queer spectacle. Her clothes were dusty and dishevelled, her left arm in a sling. But in spite of her disordered appearance it was apparent that the way-farer was no ordinary peasant or beggar of the country-side.

Tona put her head in the window of the car and spoke in English.

'If you can understand me, I apologise for stopping you,' she said hesitatingly. 'Could you possibly take me as far as the next town or village?'

'But of course!' the dark-eyed young woman in green, who was obviously the owner of the car, signalled to her attendant to open the door. 'What has happened to you? You look ill.'

She spoke excellent English, with a faint foreign inflexion.

'I've been in a train smash,' said Tona.

Relieved and pleased to find somebody who could speak her language, she began to explain about the train accident and the injury to her arm, but was careful to avoid saying anything which might incriminate her.

The owner of the car was at once gracious and sympathetic.

'What a dreadful ordeal for you,' she exclaimed.

She waved a small gloved hand towards the seat beside her. The attendant had now seated herself at the back.

'Please come in and tell me more about it.

You are English? Yes! I'm so interested in English people. I spent a year or more in London. Please tell me everything and allow me to help you.'

Tona stepped into the car and sank back in the seat with a deep sigh.

'A thousand thanks, Madame,' she said. 'I can't tell you how grateful I am for this. May I please ask your name?'

The answer came with natural dignity.

'I am Julia, Princess of Valega. You are in my country.'

Tona sat like a frozen image. She stared at the handsome, brown-faced girl who sat smiling at her in such a friendly fashion. Nothing of stiff royalty where Julia of Valega was concerned. She was charming. What grim jest was this? wondered Tona. Why had fate forced her to meet the one woman who was to be Valentine's wife? For a moment Tona thought she was going to faint. She turned so white that the princess was startled. She gave an order to her maid, who produced a flask of brandy. Julia passed this to Tona.

'No thank you,' Tona managed to say. 'I'm quite all right – thank you – just the shock of the accident. I'll be all right in a few moments.'

The chauffeur had started the car. They were being driven now swiftly through the countryside. The rough lane was soon left behind and they turned into a wide road which was heavily sign-posted. The young Princess of Valega talked vivaciously, pouring out a stream of questions which Tona answered vaguely through pale quivering lips. Finally Julia mentioned the name which Tona dreaded to hear.

'I am going to be married,' she said with simple pride. 'My fiancé is waiting for me at this very moment in my father's castle. He is Valentine, King of Gardenia. Perhaps you have seen him...?'

Tona nodded her head.

'Yes,' she said lifelessly. 'I have seen him.'

The princess continued to talk like an excited child. She was on her way back from a visit to her aunt, she said, who was the abbess of a convent on the frontier. The nuns were going to make her trousseau. The big wedding would perhaps be rather an ordeal, but it was all very thrilling. Valentine was young and handsome. Gardenia wasa glorious country. To be Queen Julia of Gardenia would be perfect. Especially as her future husband adored riding and hunting like herself, she chattered on.

'You must stay with me, Mees Felton,' she concluded. 'There are a thousand and one things I could give you to do. I love English methods. I would like my staff to learn English. You could teach them.'

Tona looked at her speechlessly. Every word the princess uttered seemed to thrust a knife in her heart. If only this girl had been unpleasant it would have made things easier. But she was beautiful and kind, and she had been chosen by Valentine and approved of by his country.

Tona wondered bitterly what Julia of Valega would have said if she had known the truth. How would this happy young woman react if she knew that her passenger had once been more – so very much more – than a conventional fiancée to Valentine? What would she think if she were to learn that Tona had once lain in his arms giving him kiss for kiss, and that he had once sworn to marry her and renounce his kingdom and throne for her sake?

Tona hid her face in her hands. Sudden bitter resentment convulsed her. Why should this handsome, spoiled, sheltered young princess have all that she, Tona, had wanted? Why should Julia take all that ought by every right of love to be hers? And why should

Valentine so coolly pledge himself to the Princess of Valega and forget the vows which he had made that night at the Silver Stork where he had held her, Tona, in his arms?

Fantastic thoughts of revenge filtered through Tona's overwrought brain. She decided that she would let the princess take her to the castle. She hoped she would come face to face with Valentine. She would cause havoc. Yes! Somehow or other she must punish him for the suffering which he had caused her even if it caused her own final destruction.

'I think I will have a little of your brandy,' Tona murmured. 'My arm aches so abominably.'

Julia looked at the English girl with sympathy.

'There, poor child,' she said, holding out the flask. 'It will make you feel much better. You will have a good rest as soon as we get to the castle. Then I shall insist upon you staying with me. I should like to have an English girl as a personal attendant. I only hope that all the preparations for my wedding will not bore you. But perhaps you, also, know what is love. Are you engaged – or married?'

Tona tried to force back the tears which

were filling her eyes.

'No,' she said, 'neither.'

The young princess drew a gold case from her bag. It bore a jewelled coronet. She opened it and handed it to Tona.

'You are too young and too pretty to be so sad,' she said with a smile. 'Smoke one of my favourite cigarettes – please. And say you will stay with me. A few days in Valega will give you a different outlook on life. We are all happy here. I want to see *you* well and happy too before you leave.'

'You are very kind,' said Tona, and prayed fervently that she would not be present to witness the next meeting between this girl and the King of Gardenia.

12

The castle of the Valegas stood on the crest of a hill and commanded a magnificent view of the surrounding country. Tonight it was *en fête*. Flags were flying from the highest turrets. The Gardenian colours were hung everywhere in honour of the royal guest. Inside the rambling old building a banquet was being prepared to celebrate the official engagement of Valentine of Gardenia and the young princess.

In Julia's own suite there was a ceaseless hum of activity. Her drawing-room was full of flowers. Her blue and gold bedroom a confusion of beautiful clothes. Half a dozen maids busied themselves putting the final touches to their mistress's toilet, and sewing jewels on to the ball-dress of maize-coloured satin which was spread upon the bed.

At the window of another big room in the west wing Tona stood looking down into a courtyard. Two men in livery had just flung open the big wrought-iron gateway. From the distant hills came the faint attractive sound of a hunting horn, and as the sound of that horn grew nearer the beating of Tona's heart seemed to grow louder and more painful. For she had been told that Valentine of Gardenia was hunting stag in the royal forests surrounding the castle, and in a few moments he would be coming back. If she stood here long enough she knew that she would see him riding into this very courtyard. And half of Tona wanted to turn and run away before she could ever set eyes upon that cruel handsome face again, but the other half, still burning with resentment, with the wish to hurt him as he had hurt her, made her stay. *She was going to see him.* And she was going to make sure that he saw her before the night was over.

She stared for a moment at the beautiful wild country-side which stretched before her gaze. On one side, at the foot of the hill, there nestled the little white town of Valega, with its terraced gardens and an incongruously big cathedral, its tall spires standing high above every other building.

Away to the right lay the Valega mountains, thickly wooded. Under several exquisite little bridges, a broad river flowed through the town. This river, Tona had been told by Julia, wound across the border into the Kingdom of Gardenia. In the summer time many little steamers glided up and down this river between the two countries, but in the winter when the mountains were white with snow the river was often frozen and all traffic suspended until the spring came again.

The whole scene looked like an illustration from a fairy tale, and this romantic little kingdom was enchanting. Tona asked herself, not for the first time that day, what in heaven's name her sister and brother-in-law would have said if she had sat down at this moment and given them a genuine account of the fantastic sequence of events through which she had passed since she left England.

She could scarcely believe that she was that same Tona who had left England ... who had led her former uneventful, conventional existence in London. She had passed through terrible things. Narrowly she had escaped a terrible death on more than one occasion. She had known love, despair, all the emotions any woman was capable of experiencing. And the end was this ... she came as the unexpected guest to attend the celebration of a royal engagement between her lover – and another woman.

The young princess had overwhelmed Tona with kindness. She would not allow her to go to a hotel. She insisted on bringing her back here. She had accepted quite simply the English girl's story of being over here 'on business' for the firm and of having lost her luggage and passport in that train smash on the borders.

Julia seemed to have taken a tremendous fancy to her. Tona had been given a beautiful suite – two maids to wait on her – an extensive wardrobe from which she could choose whatever clothes she wished to wear.

All day, waiting for the King of Gardenia to return from the hunt, Julia had made a point of being with Tona and talking to her – overjoyed at being able to air her English. All day poor Tona had had to hear that name *Valentine* – as though it were not already seared as though by a red hot brand into her consciousness.

Now Julia was dressing and Tona had been asked to write some verses in English for Julia to give to her royal sweetheart.

'Just a few lines – something about love – something subtle and charming, and at dinner I will fold it beneath his plate and he will read it and think how excellent my

English is,' Julia had laughed.

Julia was always laughing. Tona could not help liking her. She was such a cheerful, happy person – curiously lacking, though, in feminine graces. She seemed happiest racing around the castle like a boy in her well-cut breeches and shirt, followed by a pack of dogs. She was born to the saddle. With pride she had shown Tona the photograph of a stag which she had shot, and of a twenty-pound salmon which she had herself played and landed from the river up there in the mountains which was always full of the great silver fish.

She did not particularly want to settle down to a life of dignity, of formality, as her mother had done before her. But it seemed that in Gardenia she would not be called upon to do so and that was why she had accepted Valentine's offer of marriage. He would not wish her to be formal. He disliked the solemn affairs of State as much as she did.

Talk, talk, talk – about Valentine, till Tona felt that she would go mad.

She was glad now to be alone and yet wondered hopelessly how she could sit down there at the little writing bureau to create a poem of love – for Julia to give to *him*. The irony of it made her wince.

This little sitting-room, octagonal in shape, panelled in walnut and full of exquisite furniture, was a poem in itself. So, too, the big bedroom adjoining, with its white carpet, so thick that one's feet sank into its white exquisitely painted furniture, its four-poster bed with curtains of rose satin, the design picked out with silver threads, and a modern bathroom adjoining. There were flowers, books, indeed every luxury that money could buy. It was a fairy castle and Julia of Valega, was, in her way, a character from a fairy story.

Tona put her face in her hands and wished passionately that all this could have happened to her before she met Valentine, so that she might have enjoyed it instead of feeling this terrible despair, this bitter ceaseless hunger for him which spoiled everything.

The sound of the hunting horn grew nearer. With it the baying of hounds and the sharp ring of horse's hooves against stone.

Tona, every nerve tingling, turned back and looked down into the courtyard again. And even as she looked she saw a chestnut horse appear through the open gateway; she saw the rider, a slim handsome man in brown – sitting his horse so superbly that it looked almost as though man and horse were one. Valentine, King of Gardenia, followed by the rest of the hunt – men and women in pink and black. Two huntsmen between them carried a great dead stag suspended from the poles to which it was tied.

Half choking Tona looked down at this picturesque scene, unable to tear her gaze from Valentine's familiar figure. She heard his voice for a second speaking to someone in his own language. Then he dismounted, stood a moment with crop under his arm, right under her window, and lit a cigarette. But he did not look up. He passed into the castle out of her sight.

She stumbled into the bedroom, threw herself on the big luxurious bed and broke into a storm of weeping.

An hour later, in Julia's flower-scented boudoir in the royal suite, Valentine of Gardenia sat smoking, drinking, discussing the hunt with his newly-made fiancée.

Julia had changed into a smart black dress, obviously of French cut and design. She wore with it a double row of priceless pearls, and a great emerald clip. Her dark hair was wound in lustrous plaits around her small head. She, too, was smoking, using a long jade holder. She looked very handsome and she laughed a great deal, showing her white, boyish teeth.

Her brown eyes gleamed shyly but with pleasure at the young king who sat opposite her. She thought how wonderfully good to look at he was. Those blue eyes of his smiled at her and yet Julia had a queer feeling that they were not the eyes of a happy man. Even his smile had a slightly bitter quality.

'Are you pleased to be here in my country?' she asked.

'I am delighted,' he said formally.

'It is a superb country for hunting and fishing.'

'So I have discovered.'

'Although we must live in Gardenia, perhaps we can come here for our sport,' she added with shy pride.

And he thought that she was definitely handsome and attractive in her way, and that she was a very pleasant companionable girl – unusually lacking in stiffness and formality for one of her station. He would be able to share her sport and enjoy it. But he would never be able to love her. She was not his type. For all day since his arrival in Valega his mind had been pierced by memories of the one and only woman he had ever really loved – his English Tona. What a contrast that pale golden head to the dark braided one of Julia. How exquisitely and utterly feminine Tona had been with her dewy eyes, her velvet appealing mouth.

It was impossible for him to forget Tona, impossible to wipe from memory those hours on the Balkans Express, or their night at the Silver Stork which had been so full of dear, lost passion.

He had written her a letter in which he had explained what had happened since he asked her to marry him. With all his heart and soul he had wanted to keep that promise, but the political situation had made it impossible. His ministers had convinced him that, unless they had an immediate alliance with the Valegas and brought financial aid to Gardenia, it would spell ruin for the country. The letter must have been a shattering blow for Tona, but he hoped and prayed that she would understand that, even for her sake, he could not wilfully bring ruin to his people. It had never struck him that that important letter had been destroyed before it reached her.

Suddenly he became conscious that the princess was speaking to him.

'You look thoughtful, Valentine,' she was saying. 'Or is it that you are tired?'

He roused himself and smiled down at her. It was obvious that she expected a gallant answer, so he would give her one. After all, she was soon to become his wife and it was his duty to make some effort to entertain her.

'I was just thinking,' he began.

'Of what?' Her strong-looking brown fingers, on which a solitaire diamond engagement ring sparkled in the light, clung to his. 'What are you thinking about?'

'About our wedding,' he said lightly, raising her hand to his lips. 'Surely that is your fiancé's prerogative?'

Julia flushed and seemed pleased.

'I like to hear you say that,' she murmured. 'I am thinking about it too. There is still so much to be done before our marriage that it leaves little time for us to meet meanwhile.'

They stayed together for the best part of an hour. The princess talked excitedly, telling him of the endless preparations which were taking place in the castle. Finally she looked at the jewelled watch on her wrist and jumped to her feet.

'You are going?' Valentine asked, rising to

stand beside her.

She nodded.

'Yes, my dear. I must dress for dinner. I'm terribly late.'

He bowed over her hand, kissing it lightly.

Julia entered her bedroom in high spirits. She was convinced that Valentine was the most handsome man in the world. Life had been kind to her. How very different it all might have been if her father had arranged her marriage with some suitable, but unattractive man. Now not only would she soon be a reigning queen but she would have a perfect lover. He had not taken her in his arms yet, but he would – later this evening.

'You look beautiful tonight, Your Highness,' one of her maids remarked when finally she helped her mistress into the gleaming satin dress. 'I have never seen you more radiant.'

'Thank you, Magda,' Julia smiled. 'Now will you please ask Miss Felton to come here. I want her to see my dress.'

The maid bit her lip.

'I'm afraid the English lady is ill, Your Highness.'

'Ill! But why have I not been told before?'

'I didn't want to worry Your Highness tonight,' the woman said apologetically. 'Miss Felton fainted about an hour ago. She had

211

just had her bath and it was lucky Rosalie was attending her. But I do not think it is anything serious. I have asked the doctor to visit her, Highness.'

Julia took a final glance in the mirror, then walked to her English guest's suite. She was genuinely upset to hear that her new friend was ill, and annoyed that she had not been informed at once. Her anxiety was increased when she found the English girl lying in bed, her face drained of colour and her eyes big and feverish staring in front of her.

'My dear child, what is the matter?' Julia asked in her pretty broken English. 'What does the doctor say? I must see him and ask him. It is your injured arm perhaps?'

Tona looked up. There was tragedy written on her pale beautiful face when she answered: 'Your Highness need not ask him. I will tell you. Perhaps you will want me to leave the castle at once. I never expected – never dreamed, but I...'

She broke off abruptly. There was a burning flush on her cheeks, and a wild look in her eyes.

'Tell me, my dear,' the princess said kindly. 'I am here to help you.'

'*I am going to have a child.*'

Tona whispered the words. Since the

doctor had examined her this evening and told her the fact, she had felt utterly crushed. It seemed incredible, but she knew it was true. She, Tona Felton, was going to have a child, Valentine's child!

If she had been his wife it would have seemed to her a miracle – the most wonderful thing in the world. But now it was a horrifying thing. It was not so much for her own sake that she deplored it, but for the child's. The poor little thing that could never have a father. She knew what Kathleen and Tom would have said about it. They would have condemned her utterly. And poor old George! He wouldn't have believed it of her. Hadn't he always called her 'stand-offish'?

But she had loved Valentine too much and this was the price of her love.

A little while ago her thoughts had been almost suicidal. But now she could not wish to die because she had Valentine's child to think of, and despite all the agony, the difficulties confronting her, she knew at least that it meant she would never be alone again. She would have her baby to love and comfort her.

She had lain here for the last hour fighting a battle with herself – a battle which she had finally won. She had made her plans. She would go away and get work – save money and then when she could work no more, have her child in this lonely wild country where nobody knew her. Yes, nobody knew her, and she could quite well say that her husband was dead. She would go amongst the peasants. They were simple kindly people and they would look after her.

She heard Julia's shocked voice: 'But didn't you tell me you were unmarried?'

Tona's big stricken eyes looked into the penetrating ones of the princess who stood there looking so royally beautiful in her satin ball-gown, and with the gleaming jewelled coronet flashing fire as she moved her dark head. And somehow Tona did not wish to lie or deceive this girl who had been so hospitable to her.

She said: 'Yes. It is true. I am not married. If you will please allow me to stay here tonight I will go away in the morning.'

Then Julia of Valega sat on the edge of the big bed and put one exquisitely manicured hand over Tona's hot one.

'I have never heard such nonsense,' she said. 'Why should you leave the castle?'

'But of course – I must – you must think me wicked and...'

Tona stammered and, turning her face to

214

the pillow, burst into tears.

For the next few moments Julia behaved not like a royal princess standing on her dignity, judging and condemning, but very like one young girl with another, filled with curiosity, sympathy and a desire to help.

Although brought up in the narrow and strict atmosphere of the court, Julia was no prude. She had travelled, she had read extensively. She was innocent, but not ignorant, of life. And she had always been so tremendously happy. She could not bear to see unhappiness. She was passionately eager to be of assistance to a girl whose life had obviously been less happy and fortunate than her own.

She tried to stem the flow of Tona's tears. She asked innumerable questions about the man responsible. Was he English? Was he Gardenian? Couldn't she get hold of him and tell him? Couldn't he be made responsible, or was he married and unable to give this child a name?

Questions that Tona could not bear to answer. She went on crying miserably, wishing she had never come to Julia's castle, for what in God's name would Julia say if she knew that her royal fiancé, the King of Gardenia himself, was 'responsible'?

215

At length Julia gathered that the English girl was loath to give away the name of her lover. Well, she honoured Tona for that. Pityingly she touched Tona's golden hair.

'Poor little Tona! You are so pretty – I am not surprised some man has been crazy with love for you. You poor little thing! But you are not to be allowed to wander alone and unprotected in this condition – in my country. Tona, you shall stay here and I shall look after you and your child. No one will know your true story. They will think you an English widow, and you will be happy yet and well taken care of.'

Tona shook her head wildly.

'No, no. I must go away tomorrow.'

Julia stood up.

'I shall not let you go. We will talk more in the morning. Tonight you must sleep.'

Tona could not answer. She lay there broken and wretched.

Julia said: 'I must go now, my dear, they will be waiting dinner. Try not to worry. I'll see you in the morning.'

After she had gone Tona relapsed into a mood of sheer despair. Her state of mind was chaotic. She could not think clearly. This latest blow was a shattering one. Yet there was some queer degree of sweetness in the knowledge that those wild, glamorous hours which she had shared with Valentine had ended in this way. There was comfort as well as agony in the realisation that she was to be the mother of his child.

But could she lie here and allow the celebrations in the castle to continue? Was she justified in permitting this beautiful girl to marry the man who was responsible for so much tragedy?

Julia of Valega walked slowly and thoughtfully down to the banqueting hall. She determined to give all possible help to the English girl who was in such dire trouble, and already she was thinking of the best course to adopt when she came face to face with Valentine at the foot of the wide staircase.

She looked proudly at her fiancé. He made a handsome spectacular figure tonight in the full-dress uniform of the Gardenian Imperial Guard. His dark hair was shining, his bronzed cheeks smooth and firm and his eyes a little less tired.

He bowed over the slim brown hand which Julia held out to him.

'You look enchanting,' he said. Valentine could always say that sort of thing so well.

She gave her silvery laugh.

'Are our guests here yet?'

'Many of them are in the Assembly Room. Will you have a drink alone with me first of all?'

She laughed again.

'Where can one be alone in the castle of Valega?'

He looked to the right and left of him and then whispered: 'There isn't a soul in the library. Shall I bring you a drink in there?'

'What intrigue!' she whispered back. 'Do you not think the Gestapo might discover us?'

His smile was grim now.

'Don't let that word even pass your pretty lips, my dear Julia. I do not intend that in our lives together there should be any interference from Germany.'

'Valega is with you there, Sire.'

'I will get your drink,' he said. 'A champagne cocktail?'

'It sounds delicious.'

A moment later the royal pair were alone in the big library standing in front of the window which was wide open to the hot moonlit night. Julia looked at the scene, her champagne cocktail suspended in one hand, the other holding her cigarette. There was an unearthly splendour about this white moonlight that poured down from the starry sky and silvered the remote mountain peaks.

Far below the castle the lights from the little town twinkled like friendly eyes.

Then Julia turned to Valentine, who was watching her.

'I'm glad to talk to you alone for a moment,' she said. 'I feel that in you I have not only a future husband, but a companion whose mind runs along the same lines as my own.'

He bit his lip. A pang shot through his heart at the memory of Tona.

'I am sure our marriage will be a success,' he said a little stiffly.

Julia went on: 'We share a love of the English. That is important to me.'

He nodded.

'And to me. There are traitors within our gates, Julia, fifth columnists. German tourists trying to infiltrate into our countries. We shall put an end to that, together, and eventually, I hope, we shall form an alliance with Great Britain.'

'I don't want to talk of politics,' said the young princess, 'but of an English friend of mine who is in great trouble.'

He smiled at her as he would have done at a child who must be pampered.

'Yes?'

'You are a king, but you are a man – and human, Valentine. How do you feel towards a young girl who has been betrayed by a man and left alone in a strange country to bear his child?'

He lit a fresh cigarette.

'It sounds an old story, my dear.'

'Yes, but it has happened to someone I befriended. An English girl whom I found destitute and injured in a railway accident on our borders.'

'So?'

'Tonight she has told me that she is to have a child. It is my belief that the man is a Gardenian. She has been living in Gardia. That being so, could we not trace this wretch and force him to do something for her?'

Valentine nodded.

'If he is of my people he shall be found and made to do the right thing by this girl.'

Julia nodded in a satisfied way.

'I knew you would say that.'

'But why let yourself be saddened by this episode tonight when we are celebrating our betrothal?'

'Because I have a whim,' she said. 'A whim – a wish, shall we call it, to see my English girl smile. She has been so sad all day. She is very beautiful, Valentine. You are very wonderful in your uniform. I want her to see you. Let us visit her together before we join our guests. It will be a great experience for her.'

Valentine touched her cheek with his forefinger.

'The little princess is kind. I will be kind too. Take me to see your friend.'

Quickly they walked up the wide staircase together and down the vaulted corridor until they came to the suite occupied by the English girl. Then Julia knocked on the door softly and entered. She turned back to her royal fiancé.

'Poor Tona,' she whispered. 'I think she must have fallen asleep. See how beautiful she is...'

Valentine stepped swiftly to the princess's side and glanced over her shoulder. At the sound of the name *'Tona'* he stiffened in every limb. He looked across the room, and his heart seemed to leap to his throat with a sickening jerk when he saw the girl in the bed. A girl whose pale, sad face with thick dark lashes curving on marble-like cheeks was revealed to him in its frame of golden hair, the lamp-light falling softly upon her.

He staggered back, leaning heavily against

the wall. The face was clear and familiar. Could he believe his eyes, or was he crazy? No! It was true! *It was Tona!*

And even while he stood there labouring under the greatest emotion of his life, the girl in the bed stirred and opened her eyes. When the heavy lashes lifted she looked straight at the doorway and saw the two brilliant figures, Julia of Valega in her satin ball-gown and tiara of yellow diamonds, and the tall, magnificent figure of the young King in his white and gold uniform.

She sat up with a startled cry, one hand against her lips. Valentine stared back at her as though galvanised, his blue eyes smouldering in a face that was ghastly pale. For an instant Tona was convinced that she was dreaming, then a strangled cry broke from her lips: *'Val!'*

The King ran to the bedside and seized one of her hands in his.

'Tona, my God! *Tona!* Tell me what has happened…'

She was fully awake now. The touch of his fingers seemed to burn her flesh.

'Don't touch me,' she cried, pulling back her hand. 'Go away. I don't know you. You are mistaken.'

Julia of Valega stood still. Her own face

was pallid. Her dark eyes narrowed.

'Valentine!' she said. 'You know Tona? What does this mean?'

Tona breathed hard and fast. She could not speak. She was terrified of the whole critical situation. She did not know why Valentine was here, nor what strange whim had induced the princess to bring him to her room. She only knew that in a moment of aberration he had acknowledged her and revealed half the truth. But she was not going to give away the other half. No! This man had broken every promise he had ever made to her. He had treated her disgracefully. But she was determined to curb all her natural instincts, which were to throw herself wildly into his arms and tell him the entire truth. She would do nothing to hurt Julia of Valega.

Valentine turned to the princess.

'Julia, what I have to tell you will need a lot of explanation,' he said slowly. 'Something has happened of which I never dreamed. Something which alters everything.'

Tona raised herself on her pillows.

'There is nothing for you to explain,' she said. 'It is finished and over. You have chosen your path and I have chosen mine. Please go...'

Valentine ignored her words. He no longer cared what he said or did. He was conscious only of what Julia had told him downstairs. Tona was that girl. Tona whom he loved was to be the mother of his child.

'No,' he answered hotly. 'I tell you, Tona, this has changed everything.'

The princess turned her eyes upon him. Her charming face was a mask, colourless except for the rouge on her lips. She could not fail to understand. In a flash she had changed from a gay, carefree child into a suspicious woman, she was aware of an all-consuming jealousy which only Valentine could assuage.

'Come,' she said to him. 'We forget that Tona is ill. We are tiring her. She must try to sleep.'

Valentine left the bedroom and followed Julia along the corridor and down the great marble staircase once again. From below came the strains of music. Already a brilliant throng of guests were waiting to welcome the King and his fiancée.

'Wait, Julia!' he said suddenly, holding out a hand. 'I must speak to you.'

She shook her head.

'There is no time now. You must explain after dinner.'

'No,' he replied firmly. 'I am not going downstairs. The celebrations must stop. There can be no marriage for me – unless it is with the mother of my child...'

Julia of Valega put a hand to her lips.

'What are you saying? *For heaven's sake!*'

He answered her recklessly.

'A few minutes ago you asked me, in the kindness of your heart, to find the betrayer of that girl. You asked me to help you trace him. Well, you have done so. I am that man!'

'I don't believe you.'

'It is true. Try to understand, my dear. I broke my promise to marry her only because my ministers told me an alliance with your country was necessary to save mine. I sacrificed Tona for my people. But I did not know there was to be a child. Now I must find some other way out. I have a duty as a man as well as a king.'

The princess stood like a frozen image. She understood and believed him. But whereas Tona had previously been the object of her friendly pity, now that she knew that Valentine had been the man in the case, the English girl became, in Julia's eyes, a dangerous rival and enemy. Julia of Valega was fundamentally a possessive and determined woman. She was deeply in love with the King of Gardenia. She had made up her mind to marry him. She was accustomed to getting her own way. She meant to do so now. She would fight for this man with every possible weapon.

Her brain worked swiftly and clearly. It seemed apparent to her that Tona had no love left for Valentine. She had looked at him and spoken to him as though she hated him. She had said: *'It is finished and over...'* Julia faced the King with a calmness which she was far from feeling.

'This has been an appalling shock to me,' she said. 'We need time to discuss it. I ask you, for the sake of appearances, to attend the ball and act normally. Later, we can retire. I will say I am ill. It is the least you can do for me.'

Valentine nodded.

'And you will try to understand and forgive the great wrong that I did you by coming here?' he asked.

She clenched her small jewelled hands. She did not want his apologies. She wanted him. And she would get him. There was no longer any kindly wish within her heart to solve Tona's problems for her. Her one desire was to get the girl out of the castle and out of the country, in order to leave the path clear for herself.

'I repeat that we cannot discuss it now,' she said. 'But we *can* avert a public scandal.'

Valentine looked towards the door through which he had just come. Tona was in there. Poor, lovely Tona – mother of his child. He wanted to go back to her and take her in his arms, tell her there was no other woman in the world, pour out his secret rapture at the thought that she was to have his child. But Julia left him no alternative. As she said, the least he might do was to keep up some form of pretence and avert a public scandal.

He turned and began to walk slowly toward the Assembly Room. He was deep in thought. But when he turned to speak to Julia again she had gone. He guessed that she had returned to Tona's bedroom.

13

It was a very nervous and troubled Valentine who stood in the Assembly Room waiting for Julia to rejoin him. She had said that she would be back in a moment. He wondered what she was going to say to Tona. Never in his life of sacrifice to the call of royalty had he chafed so bitterly against the ties that now bound him. He still loved his people and his country, but of what use to him was a monarchy and a crown if he must give up the mother of his child?

With a set smile on his face, and in mechanical fashion, he bowed and talked to the members of the diplomatic circle who crowded obsequiously around him. And when at last Julia of Valega came back and walked to his side, greeting her friends with a brilliant smile, he was no less worried. When he asked her what had happened, she answered: 'Nothing. You have nothing to worry about.'

And she had no intention of letting the King know what had passed between her and the English girl just now.

At first Tona had refused to discuss the situation with the princess. In spite of what had happened, and however badly Valentine had hurt her, she could not bring herself to speak of his betrayal of her – to Julia. Neither could she understand, until Julia enlightened her, why Valentine had been mad enough to lose his head when he saw her here, and reveal the truth. She was in a complete daze. She had never known why he had left her in the first place in order to marry Julia, after his solemn promises. It all seemed to her wildly inconsistent and quite incomprehensible.

She saw at once that Julia's whole attitude towards her had changed. The kind, boyish, laughing girl was cool and even a little cruel. Not that Tona blamed her. She was infinitely sorry that Julia should have received such a shock. Her first words were: 'It's all a mistake…'

But Julia interrupted curtly: 'Don't lie to me, please. I know that Valentine has been your lover. He is the man responsible for your trouble.'

Tona turned her face to the pillow, her cheeks burning.

'I don't know what to say,' she whispered unhappily.

Julia bent over the bed.

'Listen to me. You told him just now that he had chosen his path and you had chosen yours. You must live up to your words.'

A muffled sound from Tona … it might have been sob.

Julia fought between her natural kindliness and her furious disappointment. She had not the slightest intention of allowing Valentine to renounce his throne for this girl, nor of renouncing him herself. She considered that it was Tona who must make the act of renunciation, and in no uncertain words she told Tona so.

'It isn't that I'm not sorry for you,' Julia said coldly. 'But you must see that Valentine could never marry you. These affairs happen – even a king is human.'

'Please don't say any more,' Tona cried. She felt that her agony of humiliation was unbearable, but the princess continued remorselessly.

'The King is a man of honour. Now that he knows about the child he might even be quixotic enough to suggest marrying you. If you accept it means that Gardenia will be without my country's help. You know what that means. The Germans will probably invade Gardenia to save their so-called suppressed minority. It would probably be the end of Valentine.'

'That must never be allowed to happen,' Tona said vehemently.

'Then you must do what I say. You must go away before it is too late. Leave my country. There is no alternative.'

Tona hid her face in her hands. She knew that the young princess was right. She had tried to hate Valentine, to despise him for what he had done to her, but she realised that she still loved him. He had been her lover. He was the father of her child. For his sake, if for no other reason, she must go – leave him to Julia of Valega.

She looked with her tragic eyes at the young princess who speedily looked away from her again. Julia was thinking: 'Men are vile. Whether kings or common peasants, they have the same cruel instincts. This poor child has to pay for Valentine's sin. How could she resist him? I, myself, would have found it hard in similar circumstances.'

But she dared not allow herself to be too sympathetic.

'Will you be wise and let me send you away before the king can see you again?' she asked Tona.

'Yes,' said Tona. 'I'll do exactly as you wish.'

Relieved, Julia could almost smile again. She bent over the girl and patted her hand.

'Poor little Tona. I pity you, but you have done the right thing – for him. I will see to everything. The journey back to England shall be arranged. You must leave the castle while the King is still sleeping. I will see to your passport and get you safely across the border. The Balkans Express will take you to Istanbul. From there I will arrange for you to fly to British territory. Everything will be set out and arranged. You will have nothing to do and I will see that you have plenty of money.'

'I don't want anything,' said Tona, and the tears gushed down her cheeks.

Julia winced. She hated those tears and the cause of them.

'I insist,' she said, 'that you take the money I shall give you. It will be in his name and you will need it for your child.'

Tona could not restrain her sobbing now.

'Why should you be so kind or care at all what happens to me?' she cried in an agonised voice. 'Why don't you let me go away and die?'

'Because,' said Julia of Valega, 'I might have been in your shoes. Now please don't cry any more nor distress yourself unnecessarily. Magda shall come to you and give you something to make you sleep. You must have rest before you start on your journey. When you are in England, I wish you would write to me and tell me when your child is born. Valentine must know nothing, but I, personally, will see that you have everything.'

With streaming eyes Tona looked up at the young princess. Jealous, Julia might be, even ruthless in her determination to separate her, Tona, from the King. But she was still very much a gentle-hearted woman. Tona whispered: 'I shall never forget you. Thank you – thank you very much.'

Julia went quickly out of the room. Tona heard the rustle of her shimmering satin dress and the tap, tap of her high heels on the marble floor of the corridor. Then Magda came in with something in a glass which she made Tona drink. She turned down the lights and for a moment gently massaged Tona's hot forehead and feverish wrists. In her own picturesque language, she crooned soothing gentle words.

Tona lay in a stupor of pain and misery. But after a few moments she felt the drug beginning to work. Slowly and surely she found release from torment of heart and mind.

She fell into a sleep from which she did not wake until it was time for her to leave Valega.

And it was in that deep sleep that Valentine of Gardenia found her when, much later that night, he came into the room which he knew was hers.

The last of the guests had departed. Julia had gone to her own suite with her women. Downstairs the yawning footmen were putting out the last flickering wax candles which dipped in the great candelabra. The ballroom was deserted, heavy with the scent of dying flowers. The castle was dark and deserted when Valentine opened the door and let himself into Tona's room.

He had no further discussion with Julia, but he was still resolute in his wish to do the right thing by this girl – the only girl he had ever really loved.

He stood a moment looking down at her. A night-light flickered on the table beside her and lit up the pale sad beauty of her face. He took her hand and whispered her name, but she did not move. Again he called her. She went on sleeping and he realised suddenly that he could not awaken her because she was drugged. For a moment he went down on one knee by the big bed, bent and kissed her forehead and smoothed the fair silken hair back from her forehead. She looked as pure, as young as an angel, he thought. Yet, already she carried within her his child. That thought moved him inexpressibly. He loved her tonight with a love that far exceeded passion and which he knew was absolute.

He whispered: 'Good night, my darling. You shall never be sad or lonely again, for tomorrow we shall go away. We shall begin a new life together and never again shall we be separated. For you I shall be so happy to renounce my crown and my throne and all that belongs to Valentine of Gardenia. Good night, my sweet ... good night!'

She stirred and her lips murmured something – he fancied it was Valentine, but he could not be sure. He bent and kissed her again and then, conscious of tremendous fatigue, he left her and went quietly along the corridor to his own suite.

But when Valentine of Gardenia woke to another day the castle no longer held the mother of his child. And Tona was not to know of those kisses which he had showered upon her in the silent watches of the night.

As day broke and the first orange glimmer of light cut across the rim of the jagged mountains surrounding Valega, Tona left the castle.

She was young and strong and after that night's sleep she had recovered sufficiently to face the dreaded journey. And she had the will power to stamp ruthlessly on all the emotions which she experienced at the thought and memory of Valentine. But her limbs seemed to act automatically in obedience to the wish of Princess Julia rather than in answer to suggestions of her own brain which was still confused and tortured.

Julia herself was up and there to speed the departure of the English guest who had come so suddenly and strangely into her life, only to leave it as suddenly.

Long afterwards Tona looked back and remembered the picture of Julia, standing there in the courtyard, a great dog on a leash in each hand, the shimmering princess of last night's ball once more the happy-go-lucky boy in breeches and shirt and a short fur coat to keep out the chill of the early morning.

She remembered Julia pressing a roll of notes into her hand, a passport – a note of instructions as to her journey. Then she found herself in a large saloon car in which the blinds were drawn, and it rolled away and she saw no more of Julia and of the enchanted castle that was wreathed in the grey mists of the dawn. But she knew that all that she loved most on earth was being left behind her. She thought of Valentine, sleeping serenely in his bedroom. She wondered what he would say when he found she had gone, and supposed that he would be glad that Julia had managed his affairs so cleverly for him and taken his responsibilities on her capable young shoulders.

And now it was to be England for Tona, and, of course, she must go back to her sister, for where else had she to go? Obviously Kathleen and Tom would not want her. In their eyes she would no longer be acceptable as a relation. They would never believe her story about Valentine because it would sound to them like the ravings of a lunatic. But she would go to them, and because of Valentine's child she had taken the money which she knew Princess Julia could well afford to give her. Money that she could spend on her child alone. For herself she would get back to work as soon as possible.

She took little note of the journey in the car which seemed interminable But at length she found herself in a reserved compartment of a train, and as it rushed swiftly through the sunlit morning across wild and splendid country she realised that she was once more in the Balkans Express. In that same train in which she had travelled with *him*. And the memory of it broke her heart. Julia had provided her with papers and magazines, with a perfectly equipped luncheon basket, rugs, cushions, a complete outfit, including a fur coat and even a trunk full of clothes. She was going back to England like a princess herself. She, who might be the mother of a king's son. But by the time she reached Istanbul she had lost some of the feeble strength that she had acquired at the castle and she felt ill and wretched again, both mentally and physically.

And now that she had had so many hours in which to think, she was conscience-stricken. She was ready and willing to pay for the sin which had been hers and Valentine's but none of this seemed fair on the child. It would be born without father and without name. She knew that it was wrong, and she was bitterly remorseful. She could do nothing but dedicate her life to this child, work for it, and in later years explain as best she could and hope for forgiveness.

In the Turkish capital she was met, as Julia had planned, by an attaché from the Valegan

Embassy. She was treated with courtesy and consideration. No questions were asked and little conversation ensued. In a short time she was taken to an aerodrome on the outskirts of the city where a special seat had been reserved for her in a plane.

Then on to Malta and Lisbon. And in Lisbon, before transferring into a British air liner which was to take her to England, she saw the first copy of a British newspaper that she had seen for weeks. And then suddenly Tona was jolted out of her own deep sea of miseries and incredible adventures into the present every-day events of the world. The old world in which she used to move. She became aware that Europe was writhing and seething in an everspreading war. She also realised with a shock that Fascist and Nazi activities in the country from which she had just come were merely small repercussions from the ceaseless blows with which Hitler was hammering at a stricken world.

14

In the small 'labour-saving' kitchen of a newly built little house in Norwood, Kathleen, Tona's elder sister, was washing dishes. Behind her stood Tom, her husband, drying up. Kathleen had once been a pretty girl, but was now washed out and untidy-looking. Her pink overall was not too clean. Her finger-nails had not been manicured for many a day. Tom Bolton had an equally untidy look and his thin pasty face wore a habitual scowl. They were both 'fed-up' with life. Both discontented with their lot, although they could see no method of improving it, and Tom had little hope of reaching a standard exceeding that of the managership of the wireless shop in which he worked.

Both were 'naggers' and quarrelled incessantly. But one thing they shared in common was a deep respect for money and a passion for the things that money could purchase.

At this very moment Tom was smoking a cigar. A cigar was to him a symbol of the success which he had never achieved in his thirty-five years and a luxury which he could seldom allow himself. He smoked it with relish while he dried the crockery, and from Kathleen's pale pinched lips there hung a Turkish cigarette – her idea of heaven. Whilst they worked, husband and wife discussed the person who had made it possible for them to buy these luxuries. Not only these, but others. The chicken in the larder. The dozen bottles of beer and a bottle of whisky on the sideboard in the dining-room. The new hat and the bottle of perfume and the box of chocolates which Kathleen had long coveted. Tona had arrived last night. The purchases had been made this morning with the help of the crisp five-pound note which she had given them, with the promise of more.

'I'm still so surprised, I can't get my bearings,' Kathleen said to her husband, the Turkish cigarette stuck to her lower lip. 'Honestly, Tommy, you could have knocked me down with a feather when I saw that taxi drive up and my sister get out of it, cool as a cucumber, looking like Marlene Dietrich.'

'Marlene gone a bit sea-sick,' said Tom with a grimace. 'Personally I think she looks damned ill.'

Kathleen dropped her voice.

'That's only to be expected.'

Tom looked at the grey ash on the point of his cigar.

'I don't know that we're doing right to have her here when you think what she's done. My old mother would have thought it shocking and as far as I am concerned I always thought Tona would do something like that. She should have settled down and married old George Oliver when we told her to.'

'I agree that she's done wrong,' said Kathleen, 'but she is my flesh and blood and I can't turn her out to fend for herself, can I?'

Tom sniffed. He was well aware that Kathleen's words were tinged with hypocrisy. She was not all that fond of her flesh and blood and she had never been particularly fond of young Tona. He knew why Kathleen wanted to keep Tona here. It was one of the points on which he agreed with her, for Tona seemed to have money. And money was hard to come by these days. Of course, they didn't believe a word of the fantastic story she had told them. Getting mixed up with a king and a lot of spies and staying with a princess in Valega and running away because the King wanted to renounce his throne for her. A lot of tripe which young Tona had culled from the cinema. No doubt the truth was that she had just had an affair with one of these foreigners who had let her down. And serve her right. Fancy trusting a foreigner anyhow! He wasn't sorry for her, but she hadn't come back expecting *them* to keep her, and if five-pound notes were going to be flung about she could stay here and welcome. Not that he or Kathleen would ever approve because they wouldn't. But they would have to sit on their scruples.

'Oh, well,' said Kathleen after a pause. 'As I have told Tona, she is lucky that it all happened while she was abroad. She can always pretend she has married someone out there, and as I told her, she will have to call herself Madame someone-or-other.'

'Where is she now?' asked Tom.

'Lying down. She looks like a ghost and really she ought to be in bed, Tommy, but she has been very nice, I must say, refusing to let me wait on her.'

A bell rang. Kathleen and Tom both looked up at the indicator.

'Front door,' said Tom, removing his cigar from his mouth. 'I'll go.'

A moment later Tom returned to the

kitchen looking animated.

'Here's a surprise,' he cried. 'Get off your overall, Kathie and come into the lounge. Who do you think's turned up?'

Kathleen began to untie her overall and pat an untidy lock of hair into place.

'Can't think.'

'Why old George himself – George Oliver.'

Kathleen's eyes – eyes that had once been as beautiful as Tona's, but without their softness – opened wide.

'Good gracious! Back from Gardenia?'

'Back permanently, my dear. He says that there's trouble – revolution or something, and some fellow is trying to get rid of the King and set up a dictatorship. It's all this Hitlerism.'

Kathleen wasn't interested in politics or the welfare of Europe, but she had always liked George Oliver and still hoped that it might be possible to fix up a match between him and Tona.

She hastened into the lounge where George Oliver, looking brown and well but decidedly harassed, waited for her.

'Why, dear old George,' she exclaimed. 'What an age it is since we've seen you.'

'Hello, Kathie,' he greeted her with a somewhat listless handshake.

244

'Tom tells me you're back because there's trouble in Gardenia?'

'That's putting it mildly,' said Oliver. 'There is a revolution in progress and in all probability our factory will be making munitions for the Germans instead of artificial flowers for the firm before we can do anything about it.'

Kathleen eyed him dubiously.

'I suppose you know Tona's here?'

The blood rushed to George Oliver's square face.

'Tona – *here?* Incredible! I hadn't the slightest idea of it. The last thing I heard of her she was in Gardia and she disappeared. I thought something terrible had happened. When did she get back?'

'Yesterday.'

'Where is she?'

'Lying down,' began Kathleen.

Then she stopped. The door of the lounge had opened and Tona walked into the room. For a moment she stood with one hand against her heart as though trying to quell some inner tumult there. George Oliver stared at her. He thought she had changed incredibly since he had last seen her in Gardia. She looked thin and her cheeks were hollow and colourless and her eyes circled with shadows. She looked like a woman who had slept little and cried much. She was still beautiful and, although George was not a sensitive man, he realised vaguely that some added dignity sat upon her. There was something almost imperious in the way she held her fair young head. She wore an exquisitely tailored suit of green linen. That that suit had been made in Paris for Julia of Valega would never in a thousand years have entered George Oliver's head. He said awkwardly: 'Hello, Tona.'

'Hello,' she echoed. And then looked at her sister and added: 'I heard George's voice. He's the one person I most want to see. Do you mind, Kathie, if I speak to him alone?'

In the past such a request would have been met by Kathleen with rude disdain. But Kathleen, today, like George Oliver, was strangely conscious of some enchantment that sat upon her sister Tona – an aura which made it impossible for one to be anything but respectful and to give in to her wishes. Not that Kathleen could understand it. Tona ought to be ashamed of herself and hiding her face. Yet here she was coming into the room like a duchess – flinging her orders about.

But Kathleen retired from the room.

'I've got to go down to the dairy. I'll get Tom to run me down in the Austin,' she said. 'See you later, George. Have a good talk with Tona.'

And a moment later they heard the chuff-chuff of Tom's Austin Seven being backed out of the garage.

George Oliver went on staring at Tona. He was very conscious now that this commonplace little lounge with its cheap curtains and covers, its shabbiness, had a new grace because Tona had come into the room. What was it, he asked himself almost crossly, that made a fellow feel so humble before Tona? What was there about her that was always so aloof and mysterious? He knew how she had behaved in Gardia and there was a lot he didn't know. He had been worried to death over her disappearance and he had to admit that he was thankful to find her back here in England. He was still in love with her – that was the trouble. And she had thrown her cap over the mill for another fellow – a foreigner – the poor little fool!

Tona said: 'Well, George. It seems like another world in which we last met. Now that I'm back here in Norwood with Kathie and Tom, I can't believe I was ever in Gardenia.

It's just like a wild dream.'

George coughed and took out a cigarette case.

'"Wild" is certainly the right name for it,' he said. 'What on earth possessed you to walk out on me like you did, Tona? Surely even if you didn't want to marry me you could have let me be your friend.'

Tona sat down on the little chesterfield and looked through the open window, and she saw not Tom's poor attempts at gardening – the straggling flower beds, the grass that wanted mowing, and all the other little houses and gardens just like it in a long row, but a scene of wild and desolate beauty – the magnificent grounds of a castle in Valega – a courtyard – and Valentine riding royally in from his day's hunting. Something caught her by the throat and for a moment she could neither speak to nor look at George Oliver. She put a hand over her eyes, then she said: 'I know you must think me mad, and I owe you an apology, for running off in the way I did, but I was half crazy at the time. And there were things that I couldn't tell – even you.'

He shrugged his shoulders.

'I certainly don't understand any of it. You say you were crazy and I think that's about it.

Gardenia went to your head.'

She looked up at him with a faint sad smile.

'Well, I'm not crazy now. I'm perfectly sane again and facing facts with a vengeance.'

'Where did you go to?'

'Don't ask me any questions, please.'

'So you still don't look on me as a friend?'

'Dear George, don't be angry with me. I think you've been immensely kind in the face of what happened in Gardia. But what happened to me is a secret which belongs to someone else as well as to me, and without his permission, I shall never tell it to a living soul.'

'Are you alluding to this fellow you fell for on the train?'

'Yes.'

'Well, didn't you find him?'

'I found him but he can't – marry me,' she said with difficulty.

George Oliver shrugged his shoulders again.

'It all sounds most mysterious and unsatisfactory. However, I'm still damnably fond of you, Tona. In spite of what I know, I'd still like you to marry me and settle down.'

She flushed and her eyes filled with tears.

'It's more than good of you, George, but

there is a very grave reason why I can't accept that generous offer.'

'Oh, I know you aren't in love with me,' he began.

'Not only that...' she turned her face from him and stared out at the sunlit little garden again. Then she added almost in a whisper: 'You see, George, I – I'm going to have a child.'

He gave a gasp.

'Oh, lord, Tona! But this is awful.'

She turned back to him.

'Don't ask me any more about it, please. I just can't answer a single question, but I *am* going to have this child, and the father can't marry me and there it is. Fortunately I have enough money for the moment and after my child is born I can work again. Kathleen's been kinder than I hoped and I am going to stay here and for the sake of the neighbours, call myself Mrs Smith or anything that Kathleen likes to suggest.'

For a moment George Oliver struggled with himself – his principles of a lifetime – his morals – everything that instinctively revolted against the news that this girl had just given him; then his very real affection for her conquered. In a harsh voice he said: 'Well, you asked me not to question you, so I

250

won't. This fellow was a villain and that's all there is to it. But there is all the more reason why you should marry me, and at once.'

She gave a little gasp.

'George!'

'Yes,' he said, scowling at the point of his shoe. 'I daresay I'm a fool but that's how I feel about you. You've got yourself into this scrape in Gardenia and ruined yourself. But I'm willing to forgive it. I know you weren't happy and you are devastatingly pretty and romantic and this is the result. You must marry me, Tona, and let me give you and the child a name.'

For a moment Tona could not speak. With her face hidden in her hands she battled with herself. Her whole heart – all that was really Tona – was still in that far-off country with her beloved Valentine. He was not the 'swine' that George thought him. He was just a man who, unfortunately for him, had been born a king, and must obey the dictates of his country rather than his heart. She would love him until she died. And she would worship his child. But by this time he was probably making all arrangements for his marriage to Julia of Valega. It was hopeless for her to grieve for him. Useless to hope that she would ever see him again. And perhaps it was her duty to take what George offered – her duty to the coming child. But at the thought that he might be brought up (yes, she was sure it was going to be a son) in the name of Oliver – he who should be a prince – she hesitated. How could she do it? How could she accept George's offer since it would mean giving herself to *him?*

'You must marry me, Tona,' she heard George saying, and he leaned forward and took hold of her hand.

She looked up at him, the tears streaming down her face.

'George ... I am grateful, but please give me time to think. Let me think about it tonight. It doesn't seem fair to you, and I...' she broke off as though she found it impossible to say what she wanted to. George heaved a sigh and dropped her hand.

'You're a queer one, Tona. But all right – have it your own way and give me your answer tomorrow.'

For a moment there was silence. Then Tona found her voice again. With all her soul in her eyes she asked George Oliver a question that she had been burning to put to him ever since she had come into this room.

'George – what is happening in Gardenia?

Do you know anything about – the young king and his marriage?'

Oliver lit another cigarette.

'Oh, that's off, my dear.'

Tona's heart jolted wildly.

'Why off?'

'Haven't you seen your paper this morning?'

'No.'

George took an *Evening Standard* out of his pocket.

'This is an early edition. Take a look at it. In the face of that you'll see that the King of Gardenia will hardly perpetrate anything in the way of matrimony. No, my dear, he'll take his place with the other ex-royalties who are now living in exile in our country.'

Tona, cheeks on fire and heart still madly racing, looked at the headlines which George had pointed out to her.

'REVOLUTION IN GARDENIA'

In a kind of daze she heard George's prosaic voice meandering on: 'The Nazis are at the back of it, of course. Count Lakost, of whom you may have heard and who was supposed to be a loyalist, has been at the head of the Fascists for years. In fact, the whole country has been a network of spies and intrigue, which I don't suppose you noticed.'

Tona did not answer, but she could have laughed aloud with irony when she thought of how she, personally, had been involved in that intrigue, and of the part Lakost's agent, Rosta, had forced her to play with Valentine's military adviser, Baron Nicholas. She shuddered at the very memory of that attempted assassination and her own arrest and imprisonment from which only Valentine had saved her.

Intently she read the paragraph that George had pointed out.

'*The revolutionary movement in Gardenia, headed by Count Lakost, established itself firmly in Gardia last night. It has for some time been known that German and Italian "tourists" have been infiltrating into the country, and that Lakost is working on behalf of the Axis. The army, under Lakost, made an attack on the palace just after sunset, sacked it and left it burning. King Valentine and his suite escaped, and it is believed that they got across the border with the help of his loyal supporters. There is heavy fighting in the streets of Gardia and a warning has been issued to the people that they must either accept the dictator-*

ship or the whole country will be bathed in blood...'

The paper dropped on to Tona's lap. She felt sick and she was shaking. She could well imagine all that was taking place in dear little Gardia – she was heart-broken at the thought of the death and destruction in that once peaceful and romantic little city. So Gardenia was now in the hands of the enemy, and Valentine was in exile? As George had just said there would be little need for him to make a diplomatic marriage. He was *ex*-King Valentine now. He had escaped across the border and possibly he would come to this country which he had always loved.

That thought was too much for her. She gave a little cry and the next moment Kathleen's lounge had faded from her sight, and with it George's anxious face. She had fainted.

15

About a week later the little house in Norwood occupied by the Boltons was the scene of unusual activity.

Kathleen Bolton was rousing herself to give a dinner party. Tona had been ill in bed for a few days, but she was up again and George was coming to spend the evening. Kathleen was still firmly convinced that 'old George' and her sister Tona would eventually 'fix it up.' She was spreading herself to make this dinner a good one, and of course Tona had supplied the cash, so that for the second time within a week – unheard of in ordinary circumstances – there was a chicken for dinner. Kathleen had made a trifle and Tom had gone out to buy a bottle of sherry.

Kathleen was enjoying herself. The *awful thing* that Tona had done remained awful, but her return from Gardenia with all this money, all those lovely clothes, this air of mystery, had pulled Kathleen out of the wearisome rut in which she had been living for some time. She almost felt grateful to Tona. Under her overall she was wearing a very pretty red and white silk dress which Tona had given her. It had a 'J' embroidered on the pocket, and when she had asked Tona to explain this Tona had put on her air of mystery in which she shrouded everything nowadays, and replied: 'Julia.'

But that was all she would say.

In the lounge, still flooded with the summer sunlight, Tona lay on the sofa with her light travelling rug across her legs. She was always cold these days in spite of the summer. And she was not well. She could not sleep. She had been through so many nerveracking experiences abroad that they seemed to have had a permanently bad effect upon her health. This morning she had consented to see her sister's doctor, and he had prescribed a bromide and had advised her to keep very quiet and let nothing worry her, otherwise she might never bring this child, which she wanted so passionately, into the world. That, in Kathleen's and Tom's eyes, might have been a blessing, but there was nothing in the world Tona wanted more desperately than Valentine's child. She was determined to get well. She would be well, she thought, as she lay here this evening, if only she could stop worrying.

But she had worried desperately about Valentine ever since reading that the young king had fled from Gardenia and that a dictatorship had been set up – a puppet State with Nicholas as a Quisling in control of Gardenia. Valega, too, had been occupied, so what had happened to the young princess she did not know. Maybe Valentine and Julia had fled together. Maybe they would marry after all. She did not know. Perhaps she would never know. But she went on worrying.

Tonight her worry was increased by the fact that she must give George Oliver a definite answer to his proposal. For a week she had staved it off. Because she had been ill in bed, George had not pressed her for the reply she had promised, but tonight, after Kathie and Tom had gone to bed, she would have to see George alone and tell him whether she would marry him or not. She could not keep him in suspense like this. She was deeply grateful to him for his magnificent generosity towards her. But she remained undecided. On one hand she wanted to give her child a father and a name. On the other she shrank from marriage with any man on earth, loving Valentine as she still did.

Tom came back with the sherry. He uncorked it and set out the glasses and chatted quite pleasantly to his sister-in-law. He, too, was feeling the benefit of her return, although sometimes he was overcome by curiosity to know how she had got this money which he was spending with gusto. He presumed that she had been 'paid off' by the man with whom she had lived in Gardenia. But Tona would answer none of his questions. The last time he had tried to pump her and suggested that she might set him up in a big wireless business she had smiled and said: 'Sorry, Tom. But the bulk of my money is to be banked for my child.'

'Did you hear the news while I was out, Tona?'

She looked at the radio beside the couch.

'Yes. I heard it.'

'Anything more about these revolutions and upheavals in the Balkans?'

Tona looked down at the tiny white sock which she was knitting.

'Yes. There are more rumours about King Valentine having reached Portugal, whilst others say he has been seen in Hungary. I don't think anybody really knows.'

'Bless my soul,' said Tom, 'there's a perfect spate of uncrowned kings knocking about the place. They're a queer lot.'

'Valentine of Gardenia was not in the least queer,' said Tona drily. 'He was educated in England and to look at him you would think he was an Englishman.'

'Did you ever see him?'

Her hands clenched. She swallowed hard. 'Yes, I saw him.'

Then she was thankful that George arrived and Tom could question her no further. She could not bear to talk about Valentine. Oh, where was he? In Portugal? In Hungary? In London? How utterly lost to her he seemed. Sometimes her longing for him was intolerable anguish.

She remembered the doctor's warning that she must not worry. With a valiant effort she greeted George and tried to make polite conversation.

It was during the little dinner party that the miracle happened.

The front door bell rang. Kathleen, who was enjoying her well-cooked dinner, clicked her tongue impatiently and rose.

'Now who's that at this time of the day? Why can't folks be allowed to have their meals in peace?'

She went to the front door. When she came back she looked a little flushed and eyed Tona slyly.

'It's someone to see you, Tona. My word! What a car he's come in. Looks like a Rolls to me, chauffeur and all, *and* what a boy! Gary Cooper isn't in it.'

Tona stared at her sister.

'Did he give his name?'

'Yes. He said: "Is this where Miss Felton lives," and when I said "Yes," he said: "Will you ask if she will see me. My name is Valentine Carr?"'

George Oliver, about to raise a fork to his mouth, let it fall to his plate with a clatter.

'Carr.' Why surely to goodness that was the name of the fellow Tona had met in the train? In other words, *the* man!

All eyes were focussed on Tona. She had sprung to her feet. Her face was white as death and her eyes looked like two enormous stars. She made as though to speak, but no words came. Then George, Kathie and Tom were electrified by the cry that broke from her lips:

'Valentine!' she said in a heart-breaking voce. 'It's Valentine.'

And she ran from the room and a door closed behind her.

In the lounge the ex-King of Gardenia looked at the girl whom he had come

261

thousands of miles to see.

He saw a slight, well-remembered figure, wearing a dress of misty blue. He saw the white thin face and the big starry eyes. He saw the pale gold head, drooping a little as though the weight of suffering had been too much for it. Then he held out his arms.

'Tona!' he said.

She gave one rapt look at him, at the tall young man who wore a grey flannel suit and a very English tie and looked just the same Valentine Carr whom she had first met on the Balkans Express at Istanbul. Gone was the glitter of uniform, the pageantry of a king. Gone the imperious Valentine bowing to his people, acknowledging the cheers of the crowd. Gone the royal suitor for the hand of a Valegan princess. Here was just an ordinary young man with a very tired face and a careworn look that went straight to her heart.

'Val!' she said in an ecstatic voice. 'Oh, Val!'

The next moment she was in his arms, locked in an embrace which assuaged for her the long agony through which she had passed. She felt his arms holding her close and his lips covering her face with frantic kisses. She heard his husky voice against her ear:

'My darling, my sweet. Thank God, I've

found you again.'

Again and again they kissed and clung, drinking in the sight of each other, murmuring a thousand endearments. It was not a moment for explanations. There was no bitterness, no question of recriminations. They loved each other and they were together again. That was all that seemed to matter.

But after a few moments Valentine lifted Tona right up in his arms, carried her to the couch and laid her there against the cushions, and then sat by her side, both her small hands locked in his. He kissed them repeatedly, unable to tear his gaze from her. He thought he had never seen anyone look so beautiful. Happiness sat upon her like a jewel flashing its radiance.

'You are glad to see me, aren't you, my little one?'

She answered in a choked voice: 'You don't know how glad.'

'It's been hell since I last saw you, Tona.'

'Thank heavens you escaped from Gardia.'

He told her briefly what had happened. When he had found that she had left the castle that morning he had talked the matter out frankly and without mincing words with Princess Julia. He had reproached her for going behind his back and sending Tona away. When she had reminded him that it was his duty to the State to renounce Tona and make a suitable marriage, he had answered that he could not forsake the woman who was to be the mother of his child. They had quarrelled and he had left Valega and returned to his own country to find it in a state of uproar with Lakost heading a revolution. Well aware that the Gestapo would speedily be on his trail, and realising that Lakost had the army behind him, Valentine, with the faithful Paul, had escaped by plane through Valega; warned Julia and gone on to Budapest. From there he had made his way eventually to Portugal. So that rumour had been true. Twenty-four hours ago he had arrived by plane in London.

'And the first thing I did,' he said, 'was to get in touch with your firm and ask for your address, knowing that I would find you here, as Julia had sent you home.'

Tona looked at him with all her soul in her eyes and for a moment held one of his brown nervous hands against her flushed cheek.

'Then you do love me? You *must* love me.'

'Darling,' he said. 'I've never done anything else.'

'But there is so much I don't understand.

After that last night that we spent together when you promised to send for me, why did you desert me and leave me to Rosta's mercy? You must have known that Rosta was the head of Lakost's gang. They were going to shoot me as a spy. Then they were going to shut me up in a fortress on the border. I escaped only because there was a train smash, and I found myself in Valega and so came in contact with Princess Julia.'

Valentine stood up. He looked pale and agitated.

'My darling, I hadn't the slightest idea that Rosta was in that gang. I sent a note to you telling you that Gardenia was in a bad way, and that my Ministers had pointed out that I owed it to my people to marry Julia and make the alliance with Valega which, although small, is one of the richest of the Balkan States. I told you I loved you and would do so until I died, but I thought it my duty to let you go and I knew you'd understand.'

'I never got that letter.'

'Rosta intercepted it.'

'Obviously.'

'And so you thought I'd just walked out on you without a word.'

'Yes, I thought so at the time,' she whispered.

He returned to her side, and, taking her in his arms, pressed a long kiss on her lips.

'My poor little love. How you've suffered!'

'You too. You've lost so much lately, Val.'

'Nothing that counts, Tona. You know me. I never wanted to be a King. I wanted what I'm going to have now, please God. An English home – an English wife – a son, whom I pray will be born on English soil.'

She hid her face against his shoulder.

'Oh, Val, I can't believe it's true. I can't. It's too heavenly.'

He stroked the fair silken head.

'We must be married at once by special licence. Then I must take you away to the sea somewhere. You're thin and ill. You've got to be made well again.'

'Darling, you've made me well already.'

'I couldn't make you a queen, Tona. You will just be Mrs Carr. Is that enough for you?'

'More than enough.'

'Thank God I have money invested over here. I can give you and our child everything.'

She clung to him, the tears gushing into her eyes.

'Oh, Val, it has been like death without you.'

'Don't let's talk of death, but of the life that we are going to lead together with our child.'

Three people came into the lounge. Kathleen, coughing discreetly, followed by her husband and George Oliver.

Valentine stood up and turned to meet them. Tona said: 'This is Kathie, my sister, and her husband, Tom. And Mr Oliver.'

Valentine bowed.

'I am Valentine Carr. Tona and I are going to be married as soon as possible.'

Kathleen and Tom stared at him, then at each other. George's ruddy complexion paled a little. He was staring at Valentine as though at an apparition. He wondered whether he was going crazy, but he seemed to have a very definite memory of this man sitting in a royal car, driving through the streets of Gardia, acknowledging the salute of guns and the cries of his people. He looked at the thin, handsome face, the imperious head, the fine intelligent eyes. Good Lord, he had seen this same face photographed in a dozen windows – in a hundred Gardenian papers and magazines.

He burst out, stuttering: 'But you – you are – look here – am I mad or are you...?'

Valentine said: 'Yes, Mr Oliver, you are quite right. I was once the King of Gardenia.'

'The king!' echoed Kathleen in a voice of stupefaction.

'The king!' muttered Tom Bolton, his eyes almost popping out of his head.

Tona, from her couch, smiled at them all.

'Yes,' she said softly, 'this is King Valentine. But as you know, his country is in enemy hands and he has renounced his crown. Now perhaps you understand why I couldn't tell you anything about him before.'

George Oliver put a hand in his pocket and fumbled for a pipe. He needed it. He needed a strong drink. The last thing he could ever have foreseen was *this* finale to Tona's troubles. The fellow she had got mixed up with was the young King of Gardenia himself. George had never felt more shocked or surprised. But although he knew that his day (so far as Tona was concerned) was over he could not help feeling a thrill of pride for her. Ye Gods! What a thought – that the girl he loved and wanted to marry was a girl whom a king had loved, and whose child would be of royal blood.

Kathleen was quite unable to take the whole matter in. As she described to her husband later that night, she was in a 'flat spin.' She held out a hand to her sister's fiancé and stammered: 'Oh Your Majesty!'

But Valentine smiled and with easy grace bent over that work-roughened little hand and kissed it.

'Please! Forget that I was ever a king. Henceforward I am just plain Mr Carr.'

Tom, having thought of all sorts of things that he would say to this amazing young man, said none of them, but rushed for his box of cigars and a glass of wine. By Jove, he would have something to tell them at the shop tomorrow. His sister-in-law was going to be married to the ex-King of Gardenia. That ought to put his stock up. By Jove! He'd give them a radio as a wedding present and put up all over the place: *Radio as supplied to ex-King of Gardenia.*'

Kathleen was now shedding a few suitable tears over Tona.

'Congratulations, ducky. I must say you've done well for yourself.' Tona shook her head.

'You don't understand, Kathie. I didn't know he was a king when I first fell in love with him, and it wouldn't have mattered to me if he had been one of the footmen at the castle. I loved him. That was all.'

'But when you marry him, you'll really be a *queen!*' exclaimed Kathleen in ecstasy.

Tona shook her head again.

'No. Just Mrs Carr.'

And over Kathleen's head she met Valentine's gaze. They looked into each other's eyes for a long moment in complete understanding and unconquerable love.

This Large Print Book, for people
who cannot read normal print,
is published under the auspices of

THE ULVERSCROFT FOUNDATION